Reckoning

R.S. Guthrie

To Garret.

What readers are saying about

Black Beast & *LOST*:

Detective Bobby Mac Thrillers (Volume One & Two)

"Kudos to R.S. Guthrie!! I started reading Black Beast and from the first chapter I couldn't wait to find out where the story would lead -- a real pager-turner full of suspense and intrigue."

Becky Illson-Skinner, *Mystery Writers Unite*

~ ~ ~

"R.S. Guthrie is a marvelous storyteller...The development of his characters is awesome. You feel you've known 'Bobby Mac' all your life."

Kathleen Hagburg, co-author of *Getting Into the Zone, a Course and Workbook For The Mental Game.*

~ ~ ~

"[Black Beast] establishes Guthrie as a bona fide talent."

Beth Elisa Harris, author of the literary blockbuster *Vision.*

~ ~ ~

"[LOST:] The Best Book That I Read This Entire Year!"

Carrie Green, author of *Violets Are Blue.*

~ ~ ~

[LOST:] "Be ready to sit for a while because you won't want to put the book down to do anything else… I will read anything R. S. Guthrie puts out. His writing lures you in and makes you a prisoner of his prose."

Gail Trish Gentry, *ChickletsLit.com.*

<u>Also by R.S. Guthrie:</u>

James Pruett Mystery Series

Blood Land

Money Land

Honor Land

Detective Bobby Mac Thrillers:

Black Beast

L O S T

Reckoning

Nonfiction:

INK: Eight Rules To A Better Book

Preface

I don't normally write a preface to my books, but I recently had a reader pick up the second book in a series and read it first. She loved the story but felt she would have enjoyed it more had she known the history of the returning characters better. I thought that was fair—once a writer has eight or nine books in a series, perhaps the need to inform the reader they are picking up book number four or five becomes less important, but when there are only two or three in the series, I decided it would be the proper thing to do to let you, the reader (or potential reader) know that this is the third in the **Detective Bobby Mac Thriller** series, so if you haven't read the first two (***Black Beast*** & ***LOST***), you might consider it. (And if you've read none of the series, it sells as a set now and you can save a couple of bucks.)

I do my best to give enough background story in any "series" book that a reader should be okay if they haven't read the prior book(s), but I wanted to respect the woman who took the time to comment enough to put this preface in book number two of this series.

In fact, my editor, Russell Rowland, told me that Alfred Hitchcock distinguished Mystery/Thrillers by two different styles. The first was the traditional "whodunnit". From page one the reader had no idea who the bad guy or gal was. I likened that to a boardgame of Clue. The second style he deemed "Suspense". That would be where you pretty much knew (or thought you knew) who did what, but it was the *getting there* and the twists along the way that made the read a good one.

I tend to write the latter. I love twists. I also love putting something right in the reader's face and daring them to believe otherwise. Because of this, however, I do work hard to make each book in a series capable (hopefully) of standing on its own as best it can.

For me, as a reader—and being a character-driven author—it is the relationships I develop with returning protagonists, ancillary characters, villains, etc. that make me want to read the books in order.

Whatever your preference, I certainly hope you enjoy *Reckoning* as much as I enjoyed writing it It is, by far, my favorite of the three. Cheers.

~Rob (R.S.) Guthrie, 2013

"The killer awoke before dawn,
He put his boots on.
He took a face
from the ancient gallery,
And he walked on
down the hall."

The Doors, *The End*

Prologue

TERROR GRIPS every person differently. To some, who had seen the brutal truths in life, as in war, it could offer a strange comfort. But Hailey Carpenter had not seen war. She'd seen plenty: addicts, thugs, unkind guys who would pay her to do immoral things in the front or back of their leather-seated cars in a garbage-strewn alleyway.

But not death. Hailey, as beautiful as she was, with the kind of skin models pined for and a thick mane of dark, obsidian hair, was from the neighborhood, so she rarely worried for her life. And she was of mixed heritage, light-skinned black enough to pass for white. But even white people from the hood had a look about them. It was in their eyes. Everyone else from the 'hood gave you that nod of sad recognition.

"Oh, you, too," they wouldn't say out loud. But it was in the eyes. Most of them would never get out. Most didn't want to.

Hailey *did* want to leave the shitty streets of Denver; people were always telling her she had the right look. "It." She never took any drugs by needle and she demanded rubbers from clients (and always thought it peculiar she called them that—she was only nineteen). She had hopes and dreams.

And this should have been like any other night coming home late from one of Kevin's parties. Kevin threw great parties. Hailey was too busy for the party life, but when Kevin was setting up the gig, she always went: great music, nice people, never drive-bys or gun thugs. No heavy drugs, so the cops mostly left Kevin and his get-togethers alone.

But there was something wrong. She thought she saw the shadowed figure mirroring her moves not two blocks from Kevin's. For a while she told herself it was nerves. Bad smoke. Some pot made you paranoid. She lived on these streets. But by now Hailey had given up on the hope it was just her imagination. She *was* being followed.

After her third erratic, non-Hailey change of direction (one even back toward where she'd *come*, a move no one would make), it was still there. The shadow. And the horror in her gut wasn't subsiding, it was building on itself. The kind of fear where you're skipping along life's timeline, for months sometimes without so much as a detour or an inconvenience, and then, suddenly, you're in the middle of something.

A car crash.

A bank robbery.

A bar fight.

A stalker.

And suddenly those months (or even years) of complacent solitude, they didn't just fall away or fade—they vanished like a Republican in a blue state. Like a cartoon with a cloud of smoke.

Gone. Your danger meter went from cobwebs, from lack of usage, from everything's just A-okay to *FUCKED*. Then you tried denial:

"This can't be real; can't be happening to me."

Then praying, even if you never believed in God a day before that, you prayed:

"Jesus, *please* get me out of this—please make this go *away*."

But it didn't go away. And your stomach felt like a balloon floating inside you; a balloon overfilled with a mixture of helium and hopelessness.

Maybe you vomited. Maybe you just *felt* like vomiting.

Hailey was now in the *worst* part of Denver.

Five Points.

Even the pimps, dealers, whores, and other street cretins disappeared by three or four A.M. around Five Points.

Ironically, Hailey had always felt a strange sense of calm when shortcutting through the bad area—the very desertion of the streets made them feel alternatively safe. Sure, you rolled the dice—most the people in her neighborhood rolled the dice every day, even Kevin—but Hailey knew other routes that were *guaranteed* to take you right past all the meth-heads who would shank you for a couple of bucks. The meth-heads were the first to clear out of Five Points when the deep of night arrived. They were weak inside and out, when it came down to it, and the only motherfuckers that walked the streets of Five Points with bravado past midnight were bad dudes. And no women.

But at least when walking through this area she hardly saw *anyone* and when she did, there was more than enough time and space to react.

Until tonight.

She picked up the pace. Whoever was stalking her was one block over, keeping to the alleyway between eighteenth and nineteenth streets. Maybe if she stayed in the open, walking from streetlight to streetlight, her mind still pleading with God to get her out of this, maybe then he would leave her alone.

But she knew it was only buying time. The stomach. The balloon of fear and hopelessness and the absolute knowledge that soon she would be—

Hailey leaned against an abandoned building and spilled her guts on the ground, orange-ish liquid.

Screwdrivers. She'd been drinking orange juice splashed in near-full glasses of vodka.

But what she didn't throw up—what stayed deep inside her, eating away at all the warmth and comfort and kindness she'd ever known—was two hundred proof *fear*.

Oh, yeah—she was stone sober now.

And she knew she only had minutes.

Maybe only seconds.

She couldn't get the thoughts out of her mind, no matter how hard she concentrated. The reports were all over the news every night and Hailey had watched them all, transfixed.

The Judas Killer.

Hailey fought the urge to run. Panic scampered up and down her spine like a platoon of angry, unruly, terrified cockroaches when all the light hit them square in the face. Her stomach twisted and moaned relentlessly inside her. The balloon swelled. She felt like she could spew bile again. She did, this time on the base of a light post.

Could it possibly be *him?*

COULD IT??

Was she honestly to be victim number, what, seven? Eight? Things like this, they didn't happen to *her.* The brain tries so hard in the face of unyielding fear to rush back to the basics. What were the chances of this happening now, here? She felt as if her number had just come up in a macabre lottery that she had no idea she'd even joined.

She couldn't concentrate. Images of the previous crime scenes—or what little they could show on the evening news—displayed in continuous flicker on the white screen in her mind.

All females. All in their mid-to-late teens. All brunette.

Hanged. He had hanged them all.

By the neck until the futile remnants of life coughed or whispered or begged without sound from within the prison of their airless lungs and—finally—just—expired.

Or did their necks break and it was painless?

The news reports were sketchy on the details of the crime scenes, mostly (Hailey knew) because the cops needed to keep some details close to their chest; details only the killer might know.

A way to root out the nut jobs.

Hailey knew a snitch in the third district, however, who was lucky enough to work for a pair of chatty detectives who loved to gossip about the most macabre of events. Post-mortem, Judas was actually staging infamous killings with the bodies.

The Black Dahlia, was the first body they found. Surgically sliced in half—two pieces, the dividing line at her navel—and her mouth cut at both corners, through her cheeks, and up to the ears in a hideous smile. He left her corpse in a field to be found rather easily by the waking public.

Hailey was fascinated by it all. She'd watched all the reports. She loved the sensationalism of it all. True crime. Like a passerby squinting at a traffic fatality, subconsciously hoping to catch even a glimpse of it; straining to see the one thing most only ever got to see just one time:

Real death. And then, only their own. Or maybe a loved one in a hospital bed.

Seeing it happen, or witnessing the scene where it had just happened, was not like simply seeing a corpse, Hailey knew. *Being there* as death collected a life due and let *you* walk away untouched?

Nothing made a person feel more alive *than that.*

Nothing.

Hailey shivered uncontrollably. The life to be collected now was hers. She was sweating through her undergarments even as the frigid night air threatened hypothermia; her breath popped from her lungs in short, panicky puffs. She felt like she was beginning to hyperventilate. Lightheaded. Still incredibly nauseated.

She glanced quickly sideways, down a cross street, toward the alley.

Nothing this time. No movement. The shadows remained just that: shadows.

Maybe it was only a random pervert or mugger, she rationalized.

With a serial killer slithering about the streets of Denver, the city's residents had, over the past year or so, been reduced to the point of viewing "ordinary" crime as a strange kind of blessing.

Oh, an assault?

Just a robbery at gunpoint?

Vehicular homicide?

Whew, at least it wasn't HIM.

A shiver violated her again.

She imagined movement to her right. Then her left.

More sweat.

The nausea worsened.

It just *couldn't* be him. *Please,* God, she begged silently.

I'll do anything. A thousand Hail Marys and Our Fathers. Don't LET it be HIM.

What were the chances? In a city of several million, what were the chances that the dark figure shadowing her every move was the worst evil the city—maybe the *country*—had ever known?

Millions to one. The abduction of the victims seemed random enough.

Suburbs. Downtown. Nice, clean neighborhoods. Some low-rent, north, south, east and west.

Nothing concrete. Like he was moving around randomly but in the randomness showing a purpose, never leaving an M.O.

Other than the hanging and the stagings.

Well she had to do *something.*

Hailey formulated a plan; maybe not so much a plan, really, just a slow-arriving realization that she was running out of roadway (literally) and needed to make a decision— there was a vacant lot where all the westbound streets dead-ended a few blocks ahead. The telltale blackness of no buildings, no streetlights, no *anything.* Like the very end of the whole earth. And when the two of them *both* reached that lot—

She knew if she broke and ran he would come after her; she knew if she deviated from her current course, he would come after her. Perspiration poured down her face and back and on the insides of her legs, soaking through her panties and shirt and jeans. She was beyond terrified, almost in shock. Her mind was fighting with itself: she knew it had to be him, yet she knew it just—*couldn't—be— him, dear God.*

She felt like sitting down in the middle of the street and bawling. Maybe then he would leave her alone. She could cry and plead and beg.

The wave of mania subsided. The growing shock wooed her and she experienced a moment of quick euphoria; adrenaline-induced hope. She knew she had to do something before they reached—

A huge black shape burst from the shadows to her left and before she could dodge or flail or scream, had her in its grasp. Strong, sinewy arms held her still and a gloved hand covered her mouth (though there was no one to hear her screams anyway).

"Shhh, shhh," the calming voice whispered in her ear. "You're trembling. There, there—it's all going to be over in a moment, dear one."

Hailey then felt a light prick in her neck, like a bee sting, and the darkness about her descended quick and mercifully.

She awoke, groggy, in a cold steel cell with one closed door and no windows, lying on her side in the fetal position. She was a foot above the cold floor on a thin, hard, mildewy-mattress that had been placed askew atop a rickety cot on four legs made of cheap wood that seemed incapable of supporting even Hailey's bird-like frame. What light there was emanated from a single incandescent bulb protruding from the far metal wall and encased by rusted, curved, grated metal. The room smelled of urine and feces, though there was none of either she could see—it was as if the particles had been mopped up without actually removing the lingering stench.

Her mind felt swollen and untrustworthy—useless like her numbed, heavy limbs. Her vision was blurred. As far as Hailey could tell, squinting through the dimness, there was no other furniture in the room. Just her makeshift bed. In one far corner she could just make out two bowls on the floor—one looked empty, the other half-filled with what she assumed was water.

She rolled on her back, eyes now closed, trying desperately to clear her foggy mind; trying to remember what exactly had happened. It reminded her of passing out drunk or stoned, waking up in a strange house, waiting for the memories to come creeping back in.

There was the party, and she'd smoked a lot of cheap ditch weed—but not *that* much; enough for a morning headache but not to black out or be carried to wherever she was without her knowing it. No. There had to be more. And there were: memories that crept about in the fringes of her tattered mind, allowing but a fleeting snapshot or two before slipping back into the shadows, unseen, unrecognized.

She opened her eyes and stared toward the ceiling. Something else. The light from the single bulb now seemed to illuminate more of the room, which was stupid. Her senses were returning. And now, near the top, in the center of the room, she could see *something*. Her eyes were playing tricks—whatever she saw appeared to be moving. Nearly imperceptible, but moving, slightly, almost—*swaying*.

She looked over to the wall opposite the light bulb and then noticed a vent, blowing a small stream of fresh air. Reaching whatever hung in the middle of the room, disturbing its inertia—

There was an abrupt power surge and the weak bulb hissed and hummed and new light exploded forth as if day had finally come to Hailey's cramped, imprisoned little world. She squinted against the brilliance, her head suddenly aching; her brain rebelling at the infusion of clarity to her unknown reality. She shielded her eyes with a weakened arm so that she might become used to the new light.

It was when she finally dared remove the arm that she saw it, in all its perfect splendor—and it was then she began screaming uncontrollably. Memories of the night of her abduction stampeding back into her timid brain, crushing everything good and happy and hopeful in their path.

"The world was all before them,
where to choose
Their place of rest,
and Providence their guide:
They hand in hand
with wand'ring steps and slow,
Through Eden
took their solitary way."

John Milton, *Paradise Lost*

1

I'D BEEN a cop for as long as I could remember, or at least it seemed that way most days. That was not a complaint. Detective Bobby Macaulay—Bobby Mac. I was born for this work; I'd no sooner have traded in my badge than I would my wife, my three little girls, or my son. And if it wasn't part of who I was when I was born (many contended that very truth, half-kidding maybe)—either way it certainly defined me then. I'd always believed that all good cops felt that way—that being a cop was as fundamental to their core personality as anything else about them. As fundamental, actually, as their hair color or their height and weight.

It was in the DNA.

Whatever the truth happened to be, I counted myself fortunate to be one of the minorities in the world— those who woke up each morning excited to go to work. I loved my job. It was not about the money. I did not stare at my paycheck each month, willing the numbers to magically transform or for extra zeroes to appear. When I received the standard city wage increase, I didn't smile or frown or say much one way or the other.

I was, in two words, completely fulfilled.

Churchill said, "Find a job you love and you'll never work a day in your life."

That was me.

The worst part of the job? You'd think the murder and mayhem; you'd think the death, blood, and gore. Sadly, you got used to that. You saw guys eating cheeseburgers while studying the ligature marks around an old woman's throat. I know, it sounds horribly insensitive, as if these guys could not care less. I supposed there were people like that on the job: detectives who literally didn't care one way or the other. Or had stopped caring, more likely. Oh hell, of course there were, because I knew some of them. But most I knew—the ones with cop in their DNA—the way they learned to cope was by shutting that part of their brain down. It was tougher than learning how to levitate, but that was the irony. Good cops actually cared so much that they had to do it; they had to go numb and desensitize themselves to the worst horrors imaginable because only then could they do their jobs.

What were our jobs?

We spoke for the dead; we spoke for them by finding who made them that way.

I couldn't eat a cheeseburger at a crime scene. I'd never gotten used to that part of the horror, but I'd learned to cope in my own way. I had a place I put things in my head. Or my heart. At times it was hard to tell the two apart, especially as a Homicide detective. But that place, it had a very strong lock, and I made sure I was the only one with the combination.

Anyway, back to the part of the job that made it most difficult for me: the crackpots. My own personal stitch in the side as I ran the gauntlet. It seemed (to me, anyway) that there were people on this earth whose sole purpose in life was muddying waters that were already quite unclear to begin with. Shit disturbers, I called them. They were not simply a bane to the police department; they appeared in every place and in all walks of life.

The sad part of dealing with these individuals was that many had good hearts; a great number truly believed that the information they had would be immeasurably useful to the detectives in solving whatever crime they happened to be investigating.

Others really were crackpots. Or addicts of true-crime television.

A study within our own Homicide Division in late 2010 showed that only 2% of all leads garnered from the public bore any fruit whatsoever. That's right. For every one hundred tips our division received, on average only two provided any reasonably true information about the case (and the impact of said information was normally nominal). Yet here was the conundrum:

We had to follow every lead we got.

The bottom line? The investigating cops couldn't take the chance that one call was the case breaker they'd been waiting for and they dismissed it. In Homicide, particularly, we were talking about an investigation where we were trying to find the person responsible for taking away the most personal, coveted, irreplaceable possession any of us would ever have:

A life.

You didn't take chances with that. You couldn't. The responsibility was just too high.

I'd been part of the Denver Metropolitan Task Force "3J" for the past seven months. Our team was formed after the third murder perpetrated by the killer known as "Judas"—a collection of twenty-five elite law enforcement personnel from a dozen surrounding Metro police departments, two County Sheriff offices, and several Special Agents of the Colorado Bureau of Investigation. I had friends in each of those departments but Garvey— Special Agent Bum Garvey of the CBI—was about the closest thing I had to a best friend. Beyond my wife, Amanda, that was, who had not retired as expected from the FBI upon moving from New York to Denver to marry me, become my second (and last, I swore) wife, and give birth to our three perfect daughters. Amanda, because of her heroism in the massacre in Idaho, had been given a cushy job in Financial Affairs which was mostly desk-bound, not inherently dangerous, and offered her flexibility in hours, including working from home over an encrypted network connection.

The flexibility to work from home was almost a necessity with triplets and I appreciated the sacrifice my loving wife had accepted happily for me and for us. For our family. She was as good a field agent—as fine a cop—as I'd ever known. It was in her DNA, too.

So she was more or less homebound, and in a little over half a year since the task force's formation, I would have felt more useful at home than on the job. We had documented over two thousand one hundred and twenty-two dead-end leads regarding the identity of Judas. None useable (which bucks even the terrible odds I mentioned earlier). A few of the leads were circumstantially relevant; in other words, they were substantially legitimate as applied to the events in question but did not provide enough detail to flesh out a viable direction (an example might be a citizen who witnessed a delivery truck in the vicinity of a murder scene around the time of the homicide but the van and its presence there checked out completely). The majority of the leads, however, went nowhere because there was nowhere *for* them to go; they were phoned in, walked in, emailed in, faxed in, and in one case even mailed in via registered mail.

By THEM.

The terminal helpers.

The well-meaning crackpots.

I really shouldn't be so jaded; I was allowed to play a part in making the lives of real people better. We'd never be able to stop the killing that went on in the world, but in being a part of the justice machinery that brought those guilty of such terrible crimes in to face punishment for what they'd done, I felt my existence was somehow worthwhile. The news media—and even the police department spokespeople—referred to the deceased as "the victim". However, when a murder was committed there was a lineage of victims that went on and on.

Parents, siblings, spouses, significant others, *children.*

And almost no one remembers the victims who would never be.

Babies that would never be born. Love that would never blossom. Marriages that would never happen. Graduations put on indefinite hold. Children that would not cope with their parentless environments and would turn to crime themselves or to doing drugs or both.

When we were unable to solve a crime—when the murderer went undetected and worse, killed again—well, therein lay the frustrating part of the job. How to face the families and friends of the deceased and tell them we'd done all we could. It happened. We had many unsolved homicides each year, regardless of how much they weighed on my heart and how furious they made my lieutenant.

And in the case of the Judas killings, we were now eight deep in just over a year and at times it felt as if we were no closer to the killer than we were on that first frosty morning.

The morning we found sixteen year-old Deena Ballou's upper and lower torsos, nude, in the open field across the street from the Capitol Building, separated in two pieces as cleanly as if she'd been born that way. I recognized the pose right away; the decedent's arms were placed above her head and her legs spread open in a clearly sexually-suggestive way, her mouth cut in a Joker smile.

The Black Dahlia.

I was driving home after a rare short shift. Only fourteen hours. Things had gone more than a little stale with Judas, which normally meant he was preparing another victim. He'd kill her—or another he'd been preparing—unless we got to him within a month or so. The profiler's best theory was that he mentally broke their will by showing them, every hour, every day, how they were going to die. But not when. Each victim had died by having her neck broken by a hangman's noose; our theory being that the victim was dropped through the hole of a make-shift gallows. Bruising and lacerations were consistent with the body swinging and hitting the sides of the contraption. Splinters were also found, indicating a wooden execution device.

The reason we knew of the mental breakdown was because he had them sign a typewritten note, each of them, before they died. Each note made a similar confession and was typed on old parchment with what appeared to be an equally old typewriter. The signatures were confirmed against those of each individual homicide victim. Deena Ballou—*our Black Dahlia*—left the first note

Do not mourn my passing. I am the betrayer, not HE who HAS seen the light.

When it is time, I will be ready because HE has shown us, each of us, every day, so we are in full understanding of the method, reasoning, and the cleansing that must occur.

I am not sorry but for what I could have done with my life instead of betraying THOSE I love.

Deena H. Ballou

Our profiler was still working on his theory for the posing of the corpses to recreate the crime scenes of infamous killings. And the Judas fixation—where they intersected.

I had my own theories.

The radio squawked out of the darkness, startling me.

"Car seven-seven, this is Dispatch, over."

I picked up the transmitter. "Seven-seven, over."

"Hostage suicide situation at Clawson and Spear. Request you respond, over."

"Mary, I'm a homicide detective. I work with them after they're dead."

"Guy's got his little girl in the house and is asking for you specifically, Mac. Suspect's name is Gerry Kelp."

"Ten-four. Show seven-seven responding. Over."

It became clearer to me what was happening on the drive over and the new theories in my head did not make me feel better. The Homicide Unit—i.e. *me*, in that particular case—had been called in by the Special Tactics division of the DPD, not only because the hostage-taker had been *our* suspect, but mostly because they knew it was me who'd gotten through to him; me who had buddied up enough to get him close to talking.

They also knew it was me who blew it.

During the suspect's interview, Manny dug into his increasingly thinning skin. Bad cop. I came in a bit later and befriended the guy. It was standard technique. I'd studied his file, found some similarities between him and me—I put myself in his shoes. If *I* was sweating a homicide in an interview room, who would I want as my friend? So I became that guy. I'm not saying I am better than most, but when it comes to working over the lowlifes of my city, I admit I do take a particular pleasure in rooting out their weaknesses and exploiting them.

Again, it was procedure. I sometimes relished it more than the others and I'll leave it at that.

Gerry Kelp was one of those rare breed of killers. Not flashy, and not stupid exactly, but so completely inept that he made our work much easier than it could have been.

As I mentioned, I caught the case with my partner, Manny Rodriguez. Manny was the new guy when my previous partner and father figure, Ned Burke, died of a heart attack over a decade back. I liked Manny a lot, and the idea that I had, over the years, become a father figure to him had not escaped me.

Not that I needed the extra responsibility but there were not enough good men in the department or the world. Anything I could do, well, it was part of the duty as far as I was concerned. As a detective and as a human being. And Manny was easy; the boy had gotten the genetics. He came from a tough background but had been raised never to let it consume him. Regardless of the pressures he'd faced. Shaming, beatings, and promises of death were just a few of the hardships he overcame to become a cop. And the surviving made him the man he was—a protector of the city where he was raised; a hero in the eyes of those who took pride in the inherent good still left in their neighborhoods.

When we arrived at the scene, the crime looked to be one of method rather than compassion. A young woman in her mid-thirties was found facedown on her own sofa. The cause of death was clearly strangulation, confirmed by our Forensics Chief Investigator, Margaret Duchamp, and also Dr. Benjamin Hollis, the Denver County Medical Examiner.

There was little evidence of a struggle, and the bruising around the victim's throat suggested the killer had come at her from behind. (An approach consistent with criminal intent and forethought.) The scene also appeared to have been vacuumed—literally picked clean of hairs, fibers, and any other trace evidence. Which would have made proving guilt incredibly difficult had the perp not experienced a total mental meltdown and disposed of the vacuum bag in the trash bin behind the house in the alley. That and the used condom in the master bathroom trash basket, slathered in his near-dry semen.

Problem was, Kelp lived next door to the victim. Neighbor, not boyfriend. So he had not originally been at the top of our list. He was questioned in the initial canvas and told one of the uniforms that he heard some noises but assumed it was amorous in nature. He described a fiancé— gave us a detailed description: how often he came by, where he worked. He practically drew a sketch for Cindy Wu, our resident artist. Mentioned that he *had* heard a couple of fights and that the police had been involved more than once.

I looked the victim's fiancé up in the system and he had a pretty long list of prior arrests for domestic disturbance and assault, three with the current victim, several others with women who may have been previous lovers.

We talked to the fiancé that same day. He had a strong alibi; a suspect-buster right there, and I don't say that like an overzealous prosecutor, wanting the suspect to be guilty. I believed there was a fundamental problem within the borders of the justice system; prosecutors looking at cases from a "win and loss record" perspective. I understood why we didn't open a case until we had enough evidence to prove it. However, the ultimate goal should always be to prosecute and convict the *guilty* party; not just the person with the best odds at putting a check in the win column.

I'd seen prosecutors withhold evidence, or at least attempt to covertly suppress it, when it basically exonerated the accused. I'd seen it more resemble a game of chess than a criminal proceeding. My belief was you wanted the person—or persons—who committed the crime behind bars. Too many DAs were professionally and politically-motivated and needed to manipulate the balance sheets in constructing a favorable résumé.

So what I meant by "suspect-buster" was that it usually cleared the suspect, which was actually a good thing if the suspect was *innocent*—the solid alibi in most cases meant the suspect wasn't guilty. Most criminals weren't masterminds, setting up elaborate fake alibis. If the guy was at work, and the supervisor witnessed such, it was more than likely true.

Kelp moved up to suspect number one in my mind. He stunk of *wrong*. Too helpful. Knew too much. He went way past "willing to share" and into megalomaniac territory. Confident he could dance his cha-cha around the police in circles and the flatfoots would never be the wiser.

My lieutenant—Elias Shackleford—did not agree. I wouldn't say he was being obtuse, but he was definitely stepping on my toes. And in my zeal to prove my commander wrong—in my own version of "making the case a game"—I tipped our hand.

During questioning in our station house, I simply allowed Kelp to see my suspicions. I dropped the façade for a moment. I wasn't really his buddy; I had nothing in common with him, and he figured it in less than a second of my own arrogance. Witnessed my own suspicions firsthand. And hell, they weren't suspicions—I was convinced the weird little bastard did it. And I let him see that. Bye-bye to any chance of a confession.

We couldn't hold him. No matter how certain I was regarding his guilt; it was going to take time to build the DNA case proving it. We lacked motive, too—other than him being a creep, and the neighbor, we hardly even had circumstantial evidence. We could show opportunity since his alibi was weak—home alone—but that was all we had without his DNA. No judge was going to grant us a warrant to violate his person or residence without something more solid on which to base our allegation of his guilt. I, of course, felt they should add fucked up demeanor and a sinister smile to the list of potential motives but that wasn't happening until we arrived at a slightly more dystopian future.

When completed, our case would likely be a strong one. We had plenty of physical evidence; we only needed a sample to match against Kelp. But we needed motive, too. Being the neighbor gave him plenty of opportunity but why did he want her dead? Detective work isn't always as glamorous as portrayed on the boob tube. The lawyers had to dance their dance and the court had to maintain its reputation as objective, the pretense being that we'd all sleep a little better if we knew people were presumed innocent *first* (but knowing full goddamned well most people wouldn't mind a little stepping on the rights of cretins if it meant making the city a safer place for *truly* innocent people to live). As the detective role in this drama,

I'd see to it that we found what was required and it would take time.

I'd seen the understanding in the suspect's eyes when he walked away. I wrongly assumed this meant the hunt was on. Catch me if you can, copper. I saw it every time we sent a suspect home that had a clue about how the system worked. He knew exactly why we couldn't hold him and he thought it was prime time funny. Or at least that was what I thought. What it meant instead? Kelp recognized his fate. He might have even remembered his own mistakes.

He definitely had no plans to do prison time. It happened. Some criminals, they knew they couldn't do time. Maybe they'd been in the joint and they knew it was not half as luxurious or even tolerable as the public might think. Or it happened often that, when cornered, some humans realized they were simply tired of life and wanted to end theirs splashed across the local news.

Either way, I misread our killer. I thought he was taunting us. He was, plain and simple, inept and scared. And he wasn't going to be coming back to the station house, much less any courtroom or behind any bars.

"Let me talk to him," I asked Len Brighton, the senior S.W.A.T. negotiator after I arrived.

"This one's ours, Mac. You know that. You've been called in as a consultant only. You've met the guy. Period."

"Everyone here knows I fucked up," I said. "I showed him our hand. He's playing the cards I handed to him. Now tell me he hasn't asked for me. Go ahead, look me in the eyes and tell me this psycho fuck did not *demand* I be brought here. How long before he has you put me on the phone anyway, Len?"

Brighton didn't answer me verbally but he dropped his stare to his boots.

"You made the call," I told him. "You called me in."

"Not me. My supervisor." Brighton considered the situation. Clearly his boss had left the ultimate decision with him, but no cop needed innocent blood on his hands. Brighton gave me the cell.

"Gerry…this is Detective Robert Macaulay. We spoke at the station."

"This ends badly, Detective. That's really all you need to know."

Kelp's voice was mocking. Still some energy left, which was good. Life had not quite defeated him. No matter how much we want to die, it is never easy when the moment comes. A jail cell and a male lover can suddenly look more attractive than the pain of death and the uncertainty of the afterlife.

If I couldn't mature that idea, he'd eventually check out. He'd asked for me. It could be because he wanted to leave his mark in my head. I'd betrayed him. Guy probably had no friends, which was exactly why I went for "good cop" when we had him in for questioning. It could be as simple as it being his time to hurt me as I hurt him. Or he might have truly bonded with me. That happened, too. I could be the friend to talk him down. There was no way to be completely sure.

As tactical officers we listened to the tone, inflection, and examined (when we could see the person) body language. We relied on our training (old as it might have been), our experiences, our psychology, and our orders. Then we turned to our gut. And maybe we prayed.

"Why make this about your daughter, Gerry? That's chicken-shit."

Brighton's eyes dilated and he instinctively reached for the phone.

"What did you say to me?"

"I said it's a coward's way to hurt an innocent little girl."

Heighten the adrenaline level. It was a delicate measure. A fine, fine line. Keep him pumped up and alive without pissing him off so much he simply went too far in the other direction and exploded instead of continuing to converse to defend himself.

So many endings to consider.

"She's not so innocent," Kelp said. There was a vein of anger in his tone. Good. It wasn't rage and the adrenaline was flowing.

"How's that?" I said.

"Too much like her mother. A bitch."

"I get that," I said. "My ex is a complete stone wall."

"Bet she lets you see your kids."

"Nope," I lied. "Two little boys. Lying bitch has them thinking their old man is a loser and a bad father. Drives me to the brink. It would drive *anyone* to the brink."

"Shit," he barked. "I can't trust you."

"I'll tell you this," I said. "And this is the god's truth, I shit you not. I am the only friend you've got out here. Funny and fucked up as that may be, I do have the power to broker some kind of better deal here."

It was partial truth. I might be able to keep the trigger-happy cops from wasting the suspect on inexperience alone. But I couldn't tell a man who at his core wanted to die that Detective Bobby Mac could keep him alive. The sweat really began to run, into my eyes, stinging them. I made sure I was out of eyesight and wiped my face and head with an extra t-shirt another officer produced from her car.

"Do you *really* get what I am saying?" Kelp said.

"No, man. I don't. I mean, every man has been screwed over by a woman, especially in a custody battle. Yeah, that I get totally. But this isn't your wife, Gerry. She's your daughter. Your *innocent* daughter. It isn't *her* fault."

"She's a BITCH."

"She's a teen; she's looking for any excuse at all to hate you. All of 'em do. My sons are eighteen and nineteen. I call them the 'E Generation'".

"What's that?" Kelp said.

"Entitled."

"That ain't any lying right there, Macaulay. Fuckin'-A right, that is."

"But here's the thing, Gerry: we're the adults. We were kids once. We thought we knew how every fucking thing worked. And your ex is using that fact, by the way—using it *against* you; just offering you up with an apple in your mouth. And I gotta be honest with you, this holding your daughter at gunpoint isn't helping."

"I guess."

"Shit, if your ex was here I'd probably get fired for serving her up to you. Trade her for the little girl."

Brighton actually smiled at that one.

"You're smart, Gerry…you know? And in a way you're right. But this is NOT the way we handle shit in an orderly society. As bad as it gets, we don't resort to hurting *children*. This is still the same little girl you diapered, fed, took to soccer games—isn't Shelly a hell of a player?"

Give her back her name. Kelp hadn't mentioned it once. He needed to start thinking about her from his memories, not from the perspective of his illness. Shelly. His daughter. His little baby girl.

"Yeah. She's awesome."

"And I suppose she got that from your ex?"

"No fucking way. I worked with her every damn day."

"Exactly, Gerry. And Shelly will remember that one day. Don't steal her chance at having good thoughts about her old man. And don't leave your ex talking to every newspaper, radio show, blog site, and tabloid that will listen that she's always been right about you. Show now how much you love that little girl of yours."

There was silence on the line for several beats.

"The front door," Kelp said.

"Hold," I said to the cops surrounding the home, raising my opened palm. "DO NOT FIRE. Hostage is exiting the building."

Shelly Kelp came through the open apartment door, trembling, and was scooped up by a female S.W.A.T. officer.

"Gerry?" I said back into the phone. "That was a good thing, Ger. I want you to know that makes me proud of you."

The line was still open, I could hear the sound of the world echoing in it, so I knew he hadn't hung up, but Kelp said nothing for the longest time. Then, in a whisper that could have been anyone's voice if I didn't know what I knew and hadn't heard it too many times before said, "Just a reminder you're still in this with us, *MacAulay*. And we're far from done."

The true monster, Rule.

Then the connection went dead.

The single gunshot from within the house didn't surprise anyone there who wasn't green as grass.

But I was the only cop left wondering who the real Gerry Kelp had been and if he'd originally been capable of murder at all.

2

Ten Months Earlier, The Black Dahlia

"GOOD TO see you, Mac," Cindy Wu, our crime scene sketch artist, said as I crunched across the frozen ground of the small amphitheater with the Capitol Building rising above us like a mountain spire.

"You, too. What're we looking at, Cindy?"

"Female victim. Uh, halved. Looks like she's in her mid-teens: sixteen, seventeen. Always hard to tell with these young ones today. Heavy ligature marks on the throat, wrists, ankles. I'm putting my money on hanging as cause of death. The rest of the team is held up in a meeting. They'll be here within the hour. Figure with the low temperatures the M.E. will need to get her back to the morgue anyway and thaw her to place T.O.D. Both sections are hard as stone."

"Jesus."

"Yeah. Worst I've seen on the job," she said, going back to her measuring.

"Me, too."

"The mouth is sliced from ear-to-ear."

The victim was cut in half so cleanly it was nearly surgical, meaning the murderer knew what he or she was doing. I wasn't making any assumptions on this one. No fuck ups. No mistakes. That place inside me that wells up for the victim really went into overdrive. Shit, I actually felt like crying. I stared at the open, striking green eyes. That was it. She reminded me of Amber. The girlfriend I'd once been forced to kill in self-defense.

I ached, and it wasn't just the frigid air.

I walked the small amphitheater setting. The Capitol Building was actually across the street but it was so large it felt like the naked victim's halves were lying on the very steps of our state's towering symbol.

My bones continued to ache. Now it *was* the cold. Weather forecasters had the high temperature hovering in the low teens. The sun was out, which helped, but I had never been a fan of the cold months. Denver was a well-kept secret; we saw a lot of sixty-degree days in the middle of winter. Unfortunately we saw our share of days like this one. A dry cold. People joked about "dry heat", which was silly to argue—the problem in Denver on a hot day was that we were a mile closer to the sun than most cities and we had over three-hundred and fifty sunny days a year. You wouldn't think a mile in terms of a ball of heat ninety-two million miles away would be significant.

It was. Denver sun on the skin made air temperature nearly completely moot. The *feeling* was easily twenty degrees hotter than the official "temperature". The sun slipping behind a summer storm cloud instantaneously erased the extra twenty, just that fast.

The sun in winter, however, was much lower in its elliptical, so it didn't bring you that extra twenty when you could really use it.

"Who called it in?" I said to Cindy.

"Taxi driver. She saw the upper half first. Thought it was a homeless drunk in need of an assist. She phoned in an ambulance before she walked over. Good thing—they took her to Swedish for a psych eval."

"First respondents?"

"Pair of uniforms from the First. Over there." She motioned to a gaggle of police huddling to keep warm next to the barricade.

I walked over and recognized one in the group right away.

"Quaid," I said, smiling.

"Shit, Mac, never seen you out in the cold like this. Not since patrol anyway."

"Fuck you."

Olson Quaid smiled wide and grabbed my hand with his own. He was the supervising officer on scene. "Just bustin' your balls. What're left anyway, old man."

I *was* old. Fifty next month. Mornings like that I felt a hundred.

Quaid owned a nice Beechcraft inboard. He had a cabin up at Grand Lake and spent every weekend trolling for Mackinaw. He'd held the state record for three years, pulling one just under fifty pounds in 2004. Then in 2007 another guy beat his catch trolling at the Blue Mesa Reservoir—it outweighed Quaid's fish by only six ounces. I knew those half-dozen ounces were a sore, sore subject.

"You still up on the lake summers?" I said. "Looking for those extra six?"

"Speaking of 'go fuck yourself'." Quaid smiled. "Hell yes, I am. Been a few since you came up."

"I'll take you up on it if that's an official invite," I said. "Pining away for the warmth of summer as we speak."

"It is. Bring the brood."

"You got it, pal."

"Guess you're looking for the boys who got here first? This is Rico and Gibbs," he said, pointing to two officers standing to his right.

"Detective Bobby Macaulay, gents," Quaid said. "He's good shit."

"Detective," the cop named Gibbs said. I nodded.

"I know you," said Rico. Not in that friendly way; more like, *and screw you.*

"Officer Rico?" I said, a look of confusion shrouding my face. He did look vaguely familiar. Not from the job, though.

"That's right. Ned Burke was my T.O. and I used to bowl on the same team. He was my friend."

"Ned was a good man," I said.

Burke was my partner for a lot of years. A father to me. He died of a heart attack, away from the job.

"IS a good man. Always will be," Rico said.

"You want to keep breaking bad, Rico? I say it's too fucking cold out here for this shit. I'd be happy to see you down at the gym, though, you feel like you want to go a few rounds."

"I used to try and get him to slim down," Rico said. "Get healthier."

"So?"

"So you were his partner."

"Get to the point."

"Just seems like someone should have had his back is all."

"I had his back every day, hoss. There's a line here and you've just about stepped on it."

"Yeah? You pulling rank?"

"I never pull rank. I walk the walk. You box? I find it a great way to settle bad blood without getting asses suspended. Like the lake next summer, *that* invite is for real."

"Easy guys," Quaid said. "Gibbs. Take the detective over there and give him your report. Rico, shag your ass over to my car. We need to have words."

Gibbs and I walked over toward the victim.

"You two arrived at the scene first?" I said.

"Yep. Female taxi driver called it in. She was really shaken up when we got here."

"Anyone else around? Witnesses?"

"No. Too early, I guess."

"You set up the barricade, taped off the crime scene?" I said.

"Yeah, we called in backup to handle pedestrians and the crowd."

It was good work. I'd seen too many crime scenes compromised by lazy uniforms.

"Good job," I said. "This place is already hopping."

"Is there anything else, Detective?"

He was curt, to the point. Professional but not wanting to concede anything else because of his partner. The blue line. I got it. And I liked him right away.

"No, nothing else. Like I said, Gibbs, thanks for preserving the scene."

"Have a nice day," he said, spun, and walked away.

Rico's words had stung me. He was an asshole but he was saying things my own conscience had whispered to me a hundred thousand times. Burke had been everything to me, especially on the job. I loved him. We try to help our loved ones but too often we're the last ones capable of effecting change. In the end I'd chosen to be the best partner and friend I could while letting him make his own adult decisions on the rest. He liked his donuts, he liked his Philly cheesesteak, and he enjoyed an occasional pastry at *Wholly Cannoli Café.*

I once heard on talk radio the guy say "I don't care if giving up donuts adds two years to my life or not; sounds like two more years with no donuts."

That didn't mean I gave myself a pass. Had I really believed it was going to kill him before he had a chance to enjoy a retirement and pension he'd earned fifty times over, I'd have put up a blockade between my best friend and bad food.

But because I thought he might just be right, Rico didn't get a pass either. That's not the way men do things, or at least not my way. Respect begets respect. Disrespect, particularly when mentioning the deceased—the *beloved* deceased—got your ass handed to you. I prayed silently that Rico chose to take me up on my boxing invite and made a mental note to reach out to him on the subject in a few days if I didn't hear from him first.

Less than twenty minutes later Margaret Duchamp, CID boss, and her charges arrived. They canvassed the area, a for-real crack forensics team that was as good as any I'd heard about. The weather made no difference to them. It only changed the methodology. Duchamp was a bitch but they wouldn't miss a fiber, not if they had to dig it from the Colorado snow with a pair of tweezers, thaw it, wait patiently for it to dry, and then go to work.

I'd seen them do it and likely they'd be doing it now.

There was nothing left for me to do here. I needed to go back to the warm precinct, drink some bitter, strong, hot coffee, start combing missing persons reports, and wait for the M.E.'s report. Once I had prints I could at least try to confirm the identity of the victim. I agreed with Cindy Wu: it was pretty clear the young lady had died from being hung. The cutting in half and disposal there at the Capitol building had likely occurred postmortem but clearly at another much warmer location.

A few days later I sat at my desk, sitting on my still-frozen ass waiting for identification because of the perpetual backlog at the County Coroner's office. On the computer screen in front of me was a travel website with some nice tropical thumbnails; places a cop could decompress with his family. Or at least that was what my wife Amanda was hoping for.

The triplets were almost ten and she felt like we needed a vacation, just the two of us. We'd gotten married after returning from Idaho an entire decade back and never did take a honeymoon. Amanda took her new FBI assignment in stride, a sacrifice fly for the team. She worked often in tandem with the Secret Service in Denver chasing counterfeiters. In her capacity with the FBI itself, she was Special Agent in Charge of Financial Crimes, which meant rooting out white-collar criminals. I was happier with all of it, though it felt more than a little wrong; why should she be forced to hunt down egghead nerd biscuits? Because she was a woman? Bullshit. Amanda was a stud. A better shot than me by far; superior investigative instincts; no fear.

But I had to admit I didn't want her in harm's way. In a perfect world she'd be at home and not working. I was no misogynist. I just loved her *so much* and I could not imagine a world where I had lost *three* women I cared for so deeply.

Counterfeiters rarely fire back.

Embezzlers cry when arrested at their office.

I knew it ate away at her inside and it did terrify me that it was not an issue put to bed comfortably but rather like a toddler: tossing, turning, fighting it every step of the way. And I was afraid the toddler would wake up in the middle of some night down the road, howling my name and pointing an accusatory finger.

I'd live with it. Selfish, yes, and maybe I would approach her first and retire early. I'd been researching a few options. Personal security seemed the best option but

Denver was no Los Angeles or New York. The number of rich folk who paid well for a good security chief and entourage were markedly fewer there in our low-traffic Rocky Mountain paradise than some other bigger metropolises.

Life was a series of trades. The sooner a person learned that, the easier they navigated the future.

"You still looking for warm destinations," Manny Rodriguez said from the facing desk.

"Yeah. Amanda still wants to try to head somewhere. Until this morning I wasn't onboard."

"But now?"

"Now I walk from my car to the office and my ass still feels frozen to my pants."

"Amen, brother."

"I am becoming a complete pussy. Check that, my brother Jax—"

I stopped. Shit. *My dead brother Jax*, the heartless me whispered inside my head and my heart suddenly weighed as much as a steel ball of similar size.

"Sorry, man," my younger partner said uncomfortably.

"No, not your fault. What I was going to say is that bastard was always busting my balls about something. He claimed I was going soft in more ways than just hating the cold. He lived in north Idaho—"

"I know, Mac."

"Yeah. Yeah."

"Nothing in from the M.E. yet," Manny said, wisely changing the subject.

"You know how backed up they are. We'll be lucky to get anything until Monday."

"Seems stupid," he said. "Us sitting on our butts, them backed up like my uncle who eats too much cheese."

"Shit I should go down and print her myself."

"That's not a bad idea," Manny said, smiling.

I picked up the phone and called Delta Swift. Delta and I did the academy together and she was now a Sheriff stationed at the County Building. The morgue was at County.

"Deputy Swift."

"Delta, baby."

"Bobby Mac, you exquisite piece of beau-flesh."

"Now, Delta. You know I got remarried, right?"

"Marital status has never been a big concern of mine, you know that."

"You still tight with the doc over there? Hollis, is it?"

"Doc Hollis has been known to butter my muffin from time to time."

"I need a solid," I told her.

"One good scratch begets another, Detective."

"I'll owe you one."

"Depends on what you're asking. Might be more than one."

"I need a set of prints run on a victim that just showed up. I know they're behind. I need to find out who this poor girl is. I swear, I'll even bring a print pad and paper myself."

"No one has reported her missing?"

"Not here. The national database is down."

"I'll talk to him. Don't worry, he'll do it."

"Thanks, Delta."

My desk phone rang about two hours after speaking with Delta at the M.E.'s office.

"Detective Macaulay."

"Detective, this is Ben Hollis."

"Doc, what can I do for you, sir?"

"I was wondering if you could come over to my office?"

I thought about his "office". The cooler gave me the willies, but I needed this guy's help and if it meant sucking it up and hanging around a bunch of purple stiffs, I could take one for the team. "Name the time."

"Can you be here in an hour?"

"I can."

"See you then," he said, and disconnected.

I told Manny it didn't sound like Doc Hollis was intimating that I should bring company so I drove to the morgue alone. As I approached the copper-colored brick building my stomach started its I-hate-hospitals-and-places-where-naked-dead-bodies-live routine of twisting into a fist and then screaming to my lower colon to go into overdrive.

I signed in and walked across the freshly polished tile floor to the bank of elevators and waited for one going down. The morgue wasn't actually in the basement but on a level called the mezzanine. My catholic upbringing always made me think of Purgatory when I pushed the button for a floor between floors.

"Detective," Hollis said. "I appreciate you taking the time from your day."

"As long as this is about the Dahlia murder, this *is* part of my day, Doc."

"Delt—uh, Deputy Swift came by earlier and wondered if I might run your victim's prints sooner rather than later. She does make a convincing argument but the truth is I had just run them and was planning on calling you over about another matter in the first place."

Hollis seemed nervous and was sweating profusely. Unusual, as the room was about thirty-eight degrees Fahrenheit.

"No problem," I said. "Talk to me."

"Shall we sit over in my office?"

"You read my mind, Doc."

When we were in the office he motioned to a chair for me, removed a handkerchief, and wiped the water from his brow. "I am not usually this disconcerted about a body," he said. "B-but this particular victim—the surgical incisions, the smiling mouth perpetrated by the massive cuts to the cheek area—I don't know; I haven't been sleeping well since she was brought in."

"I'm sorry," I said. "Our jobs aren't always easy to bring home with us."

"No," he said. "But I called you here because of what I found."

I stayed silent, giving him the floor.

"Frozen in the back of the victim's throat, well behind the larynx, was a stack of thirty dimes."

"Thirty *dimes* you said?"

"Yes."

"Go on," I said.

"I am a coin collector," he said to no surprise of mine. "The coins are in excellent condition and each predated the year nineteen sixty-five by at least a decade. W-worthless from a collector's point of view you understand."

"I'm not following you here, Doc. You have knowledge about the coins, I take it? Usually I just tell folks to spit it out. Uh, just say whatever they need to."

"Until the Coinage Act of nineteen sixty-five, dimes were composed of ninety percent silver. In fact, that's why they're so thin—so that the intrinsic value of the silver not exceed the ten cent coin itself. Since sixty-five, they, like most coins, are made mostly of copper, with nickel providing the coloring."

"Interesting stuff, Doc, but as good a detective as I am, you've stumped me."

"Most texts agree that Judas Iscariot accepted thirty pieces of silver to betray Jesus to the priests in the Garden of Gethsemane."

"Are you a religious man, Doctor Hollis?"

"Ben, please Detective. Not particularly. But there is enough evidence in the books of history to suggest that a man named Jesus was nailed to a cross and left there to die a most excruciating death and, in the least, he was the kindest, gentlest man to ever walk the earth and at the most, as some believe, the son of God. Either way, I find the facts in *this* case disturbing."

"Facts, as in plural?"

"Thirty pieces of silver and the hanging of the victim."

"Judas hanged himself after having remorse for what he'd done," I said.

"After returning the silver pieces to the high priests."

The prints had a match in the system. A suspected runaway from Toledo: Deena Ballou. I reached out to the parents—the mother, Reba Carrigan, still lived in Toledo but the father had split to somewhere in the Midwest. He'd been out of Deena's life for a while. Unfortunately not an uncommon story.

Reba took the news harder than I thought. Ballou had been missing for over three years and showed signs of drug abuse that went back even further. I mistakenly assumed the mother was already prepared for such a call.

She wasn't.

She cried and told me she'd never given up the hope that Deena would find God or Jesus or whatever higher power always cured people on television and in the movies.

Such turpitude comes from the early days, I thought at the time. *Parents instill such potential long before they think the child will need it.*

And it wasn't a cruel accusation. Young kids were so perfect. I mean sure, they had their moments. Many of them. But they were so innocent and they *idolized* you. That idolization was as strong as any drug I'd tried or heard of. Intoxicating. And a parent *had* to keep things in check. Teach them right from wrong at a core level. That wasn't going to guarantee ANYTHING in the years between fifteen and twenty-five or so. That was the scary part. But if you gave them a good core, they stood a chance. That was the best a parent could do, I had long since realized.

My son Cole and I were finally repairing a relationship that sailed downhill at bobsled speeds after the death of Isabel, Cole's mother and my first wife—the first deep love (and lover) I'd really ever had. But Cole was in his late twenties and after some years of pot smoking and other drugs (thank God nothing as ruining as crack or heroin or other demonstrably destructive narcotics), plus some reckless sexual exploits, had come back around and was about to finish his college degree. He'd lost his Division I hockey career after a drug testing, and then asked to leave Bemidji State "officially" for grades (because there was no arrest record for the drug use, it was his poor grades that nailed the coffin on the four-year degree there).

But he'd rebounded, was almost finished with a degree in pre-Law at the University of Colorado Denver. Straight As. His application for the Law College at the University of Wyoming had already been accepted. His future was shaping up and our relationship was healing, albeit slowly still.

Children—strike that; *teenagers*—sometimes come out of the hurtful, hateful years with skewed memories of what really went down. Most of us eventually realize that our parents knew best, did their best, and that most of what they did (right or wrong) was done through an undying and nearly unconditional love for them.

Problem? Some realized it at twenty. Some fifty. Some not until their parents were in the cold ground. But most eventually wiped the fog off the window and saw the true landscape all around them. The lucky ones still had time to reconnect and repair old wrongs.

And some never figured it out.

Life again. A strange, cruel beast. You tossed the dice, you took your chances.

The information I finally got from Reba Carrigan really didn't help us out much beyond confirming our victim's identity, and that was important, too. CID came back with cause and time of death but not much more:

Deena Ballou was indeed hanged—the rope was thicker than your average laundry line—good, sturdy, towing-grade; the forensics team believed whoever hanged our victim used a proper hangman's knot, which broke the neck upon impact. This meant she had likely been dropped from a distance of greater than three feet and that she did not suffer. That fact offered our profiler, psychiatrist Tag

Brewer, M.D.—a great doctor cursed with a name more suited for a soap opera star—more to chew on.

(Equally unfair to Tag, by the way, were his purely average looks. No Romance cover modeling in his future.)

At least at the moment of her death Deena had been shown some mercy. The level of muscle deterioration suggested Deena Ballou had been held captive on food rations for several months. In cases like this the endured psychological terror was a suffering that was worse than physical pain but left scars, though less visible, that were equally impossible for live victims to erase fully.

My boss, Elias Shackleford, called me in for a briefing. As usual, the man was impeccably dressed, his desk uncluttered and looking as if he'd just swiped it with a dust rag.

"Let's hear where we're at, Mac."

"Yes, sir. Victim is Deena Ballou from Toledo. Rodriguez and Trent canvassed Colfax, Five Points, and a few other hot spots. No one seemed to remember her turning tricks. Heavy drug use and no consistent job history we've found, however, so—"

Shackleford waved his impatient 'I get it, no arrests is all that means' wave.

"We're about finished with the halfway houses; no luck."

"Have you considered releasing her photo to the media?" Shackleford said.

"I'd like to keep it close for a bit longer. The killer obviously gets off on the notoriety. Staging the way he does. We've kept all of it except 'female murder victim' off the news."

"He?"

"Doc Brewer feels the profile is most definitely male now."

"How so?"

"The mercy of quick death shown at the time of death. No torture or other signs of serious physical abuse. Statistics suggest women are more probable to do damage to the vic."

"Bobbit syndrome," he said absently.

"Excuse me, Lieutenant?"

"Lorena Bobbit. Cut her husband's penis off and threw it out the window."

"Oh, sorry," I said. "I suddenly had *Lord of the Rings* in my head."

"Hobbit," he said, a bit more derisively than I preferred. Shackleford had never been the same since Idaho.

"Got it," I said, giving him a pass. Shackleford played middle linebacker in Division I and still looked like he could. I was a decent boxer but my boss still looked like he could tear me a new one, head gear or no.

"Any leads?"

"Next of kin has been notified. The mother says she was living with her at the time she left. She was classified as a runaway. She was sixteen when she was killed. Almost seventeen."

"So she's ostensibly lived here in the city for, what, three years? Must have had some help somewhere," Shackelford said.

"The mother says her estranged brother lives here. Last known address was a bust, but Trent is working on tracking him down. Guy by the name of Carrigan. Burly Carrigan."

"You think we've seen the last of this guy? The killer, I mean."

"No, sir. I don't."

"Me either. Let's get this guy before we've got a media circus on our hands."

"And more victims," I said.

"Right. More victims. We're done."

3

Present Day, two months post-abduction

HAILEY AWOKE in a different cell, this time strapped to a chair. Her head felt like it was filled with hardening concrete mix. She thought maybe she'd been drugged, but it was difficult to concentrate, to remember what were her last memories. Dinner. She remembered eating the ration of potatoes, meat scraps from the bowl, on hands and knees, and lapping up the milk.

Her captor wasn't particularly unkind. Excepting the feeding like a dog behavior.

She could not focus; she only really knew she was in a chair because of her seated position. Her arms were tied behind her back; her legs were bound to the legs of the chair.

"You're awake," he said, startling her so close to her ear. "It's time, my lovely."

"W-who are you?"

"A friend."

She'd never seen her captor. He spoke to her often through the slat he could have easily used to give her a tray and flatware. Almost kind. She felt a strange attraction to him. Stockholm Syndrome, probably, but also because she'd not known her own father and there was something deeply fatherly in the tone of her captor's voice and certain words and phrases he used. He never spoke unkindly or unfairly to her, even when she cried or snapped and called him every hateful name in the book.

"I've never seen you," Hailey said, trembling, even though she was well-secured. "You could let me go and I wouldn't know what to tell them."

"I could never do that to you," the voice said.

"What?"

"I'm here to give you a gift. Something I know you will cherish forever."

"A gift?"

"Death."

Hailey's trembling grew to a quake. Then she began sobbing. "Please don't hurt me. I want to go home."

"You weren't *home*," the man said. "How long has it been since you were actually home? Did you ever really even know one?"

"My mother," she began.

"Will never even know you're gone, will she?"

Hailey cried harder. She wouldn't. Her mother hated her; spat in her face and called her a "drug whore" the last time they spoke, over seven months past. Her, saving for college, at worst smoking a little ganja.

The man put his gloved hands on either side of her face and he kissed the top of her head. "If you only understood how lucky you are."

"Please don't hurt me," Hailey whispered again. She was so terrified she wet herself.

"Oh, baby. You aren't going to feel a thing."

The man removed his hands from her face and placed a noose around her neck. The same kind of noose she'd stared at for hours on end. The same type noose she'd always known would one day be tied for *her neck*. She'd long since become convinced that indeed this was Judas. The rope fibers pricked at the soft skin of Hailey's slender neck. The man tightened the knot at the base of her skull and she felt another bee sting.

Hailey stopped wailing. A strange calmness descended on her. Euphoric.

"Who will I be?" she said.

"What?" Judas said, thrown off, unsure where he demanded sureness from himself at all times.

"How will I be famous?"

The drug—Dilaudid, an extremely strong opiate unknown to Hailey—had her feeling almost excited at the prospect of posthumous fame.

Judas was silent for a few beats. Then she felt the cool wetness of a kiss on her right cheek and just before a lever was pulled and the world fell out from beneath her feet and she went weightless for a moment in time, the killer spoke:

"Nicole Brown Simpson."

"How gauche," Hailey thought dreamily.

Then, mercifully—nothing.

4

MY SON, Cole, sat across from me at the restaurant table, that look of discomfort screwing up his face as I'd seen it so many times in his teens. It was hard for a parent to stop parenting. A teen would say he doesn't *need* parenting and he'd be dead wrong. A twenty-seven-year-old man would say he doesn't need parenting and he'd be one hundred percent correct. The problem between us went deeper than a dad still trying to tell a son what he should do.

I was robbed of my parenting when Cole *was* in his late teens. He completely shut down, lived with his grandparents for a while after his mother died of cancer. He couldn't understand why I wanted him in my life. To that point I thought I'd done the best possible; that all I'd done was the best I could. Sometimes parents are wrong, and we forget that fact too often with our children. Simply because they lack years does not always mean they are wrong, and even when they are wrong about a fact of life it doesn't alter the reality that their belief system still *affects* them profoundly. I'd taken that truth into account far too infrequently.

On the other side of the same coin, all I'd ever asked of him was the best he could do. As a parent I could accept a C-student, for example, if that child had worked his ass off to arrive at a C grade. But Cole would turn in half his assignments and end up with a D or an F. I refused to accept that as the "best he could do", but what never occurred to me was the idea that *under the circumstances* it was the best he could do.

All I was capable of focusing on was the fact that the assignments he *did* turn in, he averaged a *ninety-five percent score.*

D's and F's were absolutely *not* the best my son could do. Not even in the same neighborhood. So I rode him. And rode him. I preached the sermon of the bewildered parent a hundred times. Rinse and repeat.

They say the definition of insanity is doing the same thing over and over expecting a different result.

The lies he began to tell—in part to appease me, in part to simply avoid the "same old conversations"—totally destroyed me. A child does not understand the significance of a lie, no more than the toddler understands the significance of a hot surface until they touch it. You cannot touch a lie; it is a completely intangible thing and, in the end, something I was both incapable of accepting and incapable of explaining to my son.

I remember the first lie he ever told me—I don't mean the four-year-old saying he didn't eat the cookie; I'm talking "look me in the eye and tell me the truth, no matter what the truth is, and we can work this out" and him looking me straight in the eye and lying completely, without a second thought or so much as a pause in his breathing.

I've had many a perp who could not lie as soundly as that.

It is also impossible to make a child understand that the one thousandth lie cuts as deeply as the first. I no longer remembered all of them, of course. The lies, too, became one thick, storm-filled cloud where the lightning could strike you from anywhere at any time.

We eventually made amends. The prodigal son returned, the father with (mostly) open arms. The younger we are, the more forgiveness seems to come with little or no cost. As we age we become petrified in our viewpoints, so much less capable of letting go of the past. But as I said, we made amends and by that time in our lives took on roles more peer-like than father and son—those years were gone and I could never have them back. It didn't stop me, however, from being a parent.

The current impasse had to do with Cole's acceptance at the Law College at the University of Wyoming, just across the Colorado northern border, about a hundred and thirty or forty miles north. Out of the blue, my son didn't think UW was prestigious enough. Admittedly he had applied himself at Denver Metro, worked his way into the University of Colorado system, and yes, finally graduated with honors. But it wasn't as if he'd aced Harvard or Stanford or NYU.

"Wyoming is a decent school," I said. "They broke the top one hundred a couple years back. Firms would respect a J.D. from that school."

"*That's* exactly what I am talking about," Cole said, poking at his chicken. "You don't pay attention. I want to go *east*."

"Because the schools are better?"

"That's part of the reason."

"Cole, what's going on? You need to talk to me. Be honest."

"I can't," he admitted. "I don't know how to talk to you."

"Whose fault is that?" I said.

"See—it's always about fault and blame with you."

He was right. But I didn't understand his thought processes any better now than when he was fifteen or sixteen. Here's something I learned long before my son was in diapers:

There *is* right and wrong. Always. I didn't believe in black and white—extremes—but the truth was different.

Something either happened or it didn't. A conversation took place, certain things were said, or they weren't.

In every argument, in every courtroom, and in every decision. Yes, there were always two sides to a story. And there were *degrees* of correctness. The challenge should be *finding* the right answer. Or the most correct. The most logical, or the better financial decision. But teens—and it seemed to me, Cole, still—landed on a square patch of ground and no matter what or who or how circumstances put them there, defended it to the death.

I, on the other hand, just wanted to know the facts. The truth. And the truth had long ago become vaporous between us when it mattered most. I told him the Golden Rule when he was younger. I said, "You can lie, and lie again, but the day you lose another person's *trust*, it is over. Even if that person *wants* to believe you, they can't. They'll never know if the words coming out of your mouth are the real thing or another untruth, molded to your own designs. Once that happens, the choice is taken from the one who's been lied to so much. They might even try, but it is then out of their control."

It didn't help that Cole was the best liar I'd ever known (and that was saying a truckload, me being a cop—all we did day in and out, it seemed, was deal with seasoned liars). Cole could look me in the eye, tell an elaborate story, and hook me like a big, fat trout skimming the surface of a placid lake, watching for bugs. I bit every time. For a while.

"I'm sorry," I said. "I just want to know why the school you applied to is suddenly not right for you. I think it's a fair question."

Cole nodded. "It *is* a fair question. You're right."

Telling me what I wanted to hear. Like a fighter softening the other with body blows and hidden kidney shots.

"Talk to me, Cole. I swear, I'll shut up and listen."

"I want to go to Fordham. In New York."

"Fordham Law?" I said, trying not to sound incredulous.

"Yes."

"Pal, Fordham is top twenty or thirty in the country."

"I know."

"Colorado is ranked around fifty and they turned down your app. Your *in state* application."

"I *know*."

I stopped for a moment. I'd heard these short, non-informative answers before. There was most definitely something else happening; something was being withheld. Time to quit dancing.

"Fordham has a helluva Master's program in Social Services, don't they?" I said. I was a detective; did he really expect I would come into the conversation with no hole cards at all?

"I love her, dad. I really do. Like you and mom."

"Her" was Brianne Finnegan. They'd been dating for three years; met at a class he took at the University of Denver, where Amber used to teach and where Brianne was finishing her undergrad degree in Social Science. Cole *did* look like I did when I first met Isabel.

Stunned, almost. Reverent. In love.

I remembered Isabel for the first time in a while—*allowed myself the memories of my first honest love*—and yes, the feelings I had for Isabel were far more than overwhelming. They were a living part of me. When she died it was as if they severed all my limbs.

"If you can get accepted," I told Cole, taking a large bite of my hoagie, "we'll figure out a way."

Cole's eyes brightened and he waited a breath, wanting to make sure, no doubt, he'd heard what he thought he'd heard.

"Thank you," he managed.

"If you aren't going to eat that here," I said, pointing at his plate of Alfredo, "take it home and promise me you'll warm it up later for you and Bri."

The next morning Hailey Carpenter's corpse was found on the sidewalk in front of a home in Cherry Hills Estates, the closest thing Denver had to a luxurious Southern California neighborhood like Brentwood. A corporate VP walking outside to head off to work found the two bodies lying inside his gate.

One male and one female victim. After dropping his coffee cup and throwing up the previous few swallows, the man called 9-1-1.

Hailey Carpenter exhibited the same ligature and rope burns on the neck as the previous victims. She was stabbed twenty-two times in the head, postmortem, and her throat had a full gash from one side to the other. The fucking sick bastard had even incised her C3 vertebrae, all reported in the Nicole Brown Simpson autopsy in 1994.

The young man—Stan Perry, 27—was a pizza delivery employee called to the address twenty minutes before Judas positioned Hailey Carpenter's body; our team believed he was murdered after her body was placed due to blood spatter on the woman's corpse matching Perry's and the differences in post-mortem signs of T.O.D.

"When did the call come in at the pizza place," I asked Manny. He flipped through the last few pages of notes.

"According to the manager, who checked the tickets himself, around eight-forty P.M. M.E. puts time of death of the delivery guy at between nine and nine-thirty. The homeowner confirms that he did not make any calls to the pizza joint."

"Incoming phone number?" I said.

"Traces to a burner. But we caught a break. Serial number tracks back to a lot received at a 7-11 store near the crime scene. Judas may have picked up the cell on the way to the Cherry Hills home."

"Video surveillance?"

"Just getting ready to make the drive. Owner says they keep only twenty-four hours on tape—can you believe they still use tape? I got to him in time. We can watch all the video from four differently-angled cameras."

"It's a long shot," I said.

"In the dark."

"I'd prefer something more solid."

"Like the movie *Se7en*? Perp walks into the station house and delivers himself up to you personally?" Manny said, smiling.

"You a movie buff?"

"Aw, you never asked me such a personal question before, boss."

"Fuck you."

"Love 'em," Manny said. "Can't get enough."

"You should read more," I told him, as I probably told my son too many times. The overbearing father.

"Why buy a cow when you get the milk for free?"

"What? *That's* why you should read more. Not only is the proverb misquoted, it is a terrible metaphor."

"I could never tell the difference," Manny said.

"Between—"

"Metaphors, similes, proverbs, etcetera."

"Ah, me either," I laughed. "Pretty sure you were shooting for a metaphor, though. I got it. Movies are like Cliff Notes."

"Fucking nice metaphor, boss."

"I think that was a simile. Let's go for a drive."

"Bingo," Manny said.

I grabbed my jacket and Manny, his too. "The answer is no, by the way."

"To what?"

"I would *not* like my perp to deliver himself up as in *Se7en*, a movie I *love*, mi amigo. One, too fucking easy. I love the job."

"Two?"

"Gruesome fucking ending, wouldn't you say?"

"Amen to that."

We thought we'd have to sit in a cramped, cigarette-smelling office watching low-grade video on a three-inch screen. Turns out the manager was just using a euphemism. "Tape." Like calling CD's "records" kind of deal. This man was a techie and had convinced the owner to buy state-of-the-art digital surveillance. And he meant he duped off each twenty-four hour day from the system hard drive to an online service that secured and backed up the data. Another cost he'd talked the boss into.

As we walked into the store the manager popped up out of his office and greeted us with a nice USB drive with twenty-four hours of surveillance, in case we wanted all of it.

"It's all time-stamped, high def, and I clipped off a segment two hours before and two hours after. A little less for my men in blue to have to sift. Used a sweet little program I downloaded."

I accepted the small drive, still amazed at the constant collusion between Big Software and Big Storage. *I'll make my software bigger, you sell more space.* Chicken and the egg but you could buy a shitload of storage for a buck and put it on a piece of plastic no bigger than your thumb (although I had monster thumbs).

"Thanks, uh, Chuck, right?" I said. He nodded, eyes dancing a tad, clearly enthusiastic to be part of an honest-to-Pete homicide investigation; biggest the city had ever known, though we hadn't told him that much. "Your boss pay for the video clipping software, too," I joked with him.

"Ah, free download. Twenty-nine ninety-five if I want to 'appreciate' the private developer's work. It's great software and fuck if I don't appreciate an honest person trying to make an honest living."

"So you're saying the boss paid, he just doesn't know it."

"Chicken scratch, my main man."

"I got it," I told him. "Seriously, though, we really appreciate your cooperation, Chuck."

"Go get the bad guy, Detectives."

As we were leaving the store, my cell rang. Blocked number.

"Hello?" I said. Never give out anything until you know who you're talking to.

"Bobeeeee."

I froze. Whatever was in my stomach dropped straight into my bowels. I felt the urge to vomit. I couldn't speak. I mean *I literally couldn't speak.*

A voice from the past.

The killer delivering himself up on a silver platter.

"A little like the movie *Se7en*, wouldn't ya say, old buddy? You remember the scene: the detectives stumble upon the killer's apartment and he comes up the stairs carrying groceries at the far end of the hall while they're knocking on *his* door. *Great scene.* Perfect cinematography. The distance down the hall, the silhouette, the killer's hat and *him holding a sack of groceries.* Ah, gives me chills. Don't worry, though, I don't plan to open fire on you. Although I could."

I started spinning, looking around, eyeing every street person, every shopper, teen, hippie, homeless guy— *anyone.*

Just like the fucking movies.

"What's up?" Manny said, still finishing a Coney dog he bought inside while I was chatting with the manager.

"You don't have to say anything, Mac. And stop spinning around like a cliché. We're cool. You won't find me. You think I'd stand behind you? It's not going to work out that way."

"Fuck you, Spence. Where the hell have you been all these years?"

Manny dropped his hotdog, chili and cheese splattering on the scorching asphalt at our feet.

Spencer Grant and his daughter Melissa dropped off the edge of the planet ten years ago. That was just after him informing me he was in Denver then, not the panhandle of Idaho where he murdered his wife and other daughter, saving Melissa for God knew what.

Ten years we'd not heard a thing; ten years no one resembling Melissa had ever been credibly reported. APBs, BOLOs, the works. Spence was even on the FBI's Ten Most Wanted List, *in every post office*. Plenty of crank reports but not one legitimate sighting of either of them.

I swore to God above I never even *thought* of him as a suspect. Bad detective work, yes, but no surprise, I was sure, to a psychologist. As every year passed with no sightings, no more hauntings, demons—no Father Rule. My brain was just pleased as shit-cake to bury all that had happened in the distant past so fucking deep I'd need an oil derrick to bring it to the surface.

"I've been here in Denver, Mac. You know that. I told you myself when you were tossing the ball to your cute pups. How are the mutts?"

Tina and Sketch. My beloved Jack Russells. Sketch grew a tumor when he was just ten. I had to put him down. Tina was never the same and developed a sympathetic tumor just a few months later. Without warning, I lost both my dogs within three months of each other.

"It's been you," I said softly.

"I can't believe you didn't do the math on that one, my long lost friend," Spence said. The tone in my voice had given my lack of suspicions away. What was this, Bad Detective Day?

"I considered it," I lied. "Figured since we'd not heard from you that you had a change of heart and took Melissa somewhere nice."

"Denver's nice."

"Not with bodies piling up it's not. Terrible thing for a child to hear about."

"Or live through."

"What?" I said.

"You were probably thinking, *or to live through.* The thing up in Idaho."

The thing. What a psycho douchebag.

"Let's grab a coffee, *old friend,*" I said.

"Ha, good one, Mac. I'll be in touch. Oh, almost forgot, buddy: Jax says 'hey'."

The call went dead. So did my soul.

"Was that who I think it was?" Manny said, breaking the stony silence, his Puerto Rican skin almost as pale as mine.

"Yeah."

"You never thought—"

"No. It was *ten years* ago he called me and said he was here, in Denver."

"I know."

"I haven't heard a thing since then."

"Sure, I got it."

"Ten years."

"I know, Bobby. I'm sorry. That hurt never goes away."

The things people say. I stopped saying them a long time ago. They don't help the bereaved; they don't console the lost. I missed my brother *every single minute of every day.* His absence from the world left a void in my heart that could not *accept* any other substance, much less be filled. It was of no consequence that we hardly spoke when he lived in Idaho; hadn't spoken until—

It mattered not. He was my de facto best friend. In good and bad times. In laughter and silence. Even years of silence and a thousand miles. It went *unspoken*. Not only my blood. My *brother*. The only one I'd ever had. He knew things from the time he could remember at five or six through our high school and college years (and even some adult) that no one else in the world knew.

And now he was not of this earth. I wasn't convinced he was dead; that was from the part of me that remembered all the crazy shit that went down on that mountain ledge, the part of me that couldn't let go of it.

Ten years.

A lot of denial builds up over ten years.

"No," I said to Manny. Acknowledging his useless words. Politely. It's what we do.

"I-I just thought. Shit, I had no idea what I thought."

"You thought *why the fuck didn't the senior detective on this case even SUSPECT a mass murderer capable of killing his own wife and child?*"

"Shit, brother, I never made the connection either. I never brought him up. With the APBs, BOLOs—how does a guy stay in the city with a growing daughter and not get nabbed?"

"I should've known this had his greasy, evil hands all over it."

"Nope. Not letting you take the fall on this one, boss."

"You're a good kid, Manny. And I appreciate you having my back more than you know. But let me talk to Shackleford. Alone."

I dropped Manny at the shop with strict instructions to tactfully avoid any deep discussions with the lieutenant (Manny's poker face sucked; we were working on that at the regular every-other-Thursday cop game.) He was to get them to look at the call; it would no doubt be a burner or a tossed SIM or both. He could then start going over the video, especially now that we *probably* knew who we were after—or at least who our number one suspect now was. In detective work you learned not to jump too fast and you learned it painfully. I was taking the rest of the afternoon on personal time. I needed to think, clear my head.

I took Granger, my new Border Collie, to the same dog park near my home where Spence Grant called me all those years ago. Granger was a sweetie. She was three now. It took me a while to get over grieving Tina and Sketch. I'd never own another Russell again. Those two were that special.

And god I loved the energy Granger brought to the house. She *adored* the triplets. Amanda was not a huge dog person—which primarily meant she did not grow up around them—but she and Granger were inseparable at times; enough, even, to make me jealous. Amanda was home all day with her much of the time; raised her when she was a piddling-on-the-carpet puppy, so it was inevitable.

Borders were *smart*, like Russells. She helped with the kids more than she hurt. Amanda trained her to pick up clothes and put them in the laundry room basket, watch and warn for any crying when the girls were out of earshot, and a slew of other great jobs that amazed me. I only ever played ball with Tina and Sketch, though they loved me as much as I ever loved them.

As I threw the Frisbee for Granger, I tried to reach my Zen *anapanasati,* a consciousness of in and out breathing. I picked up on Zen practice a few years back. The only path to calm for me then, and I really needed to reprogram and rearrange the mind and all it had been accumulating the past few years.

Jax.

God I had tried so hard over the years to come to grips—or at least a peaceful understanding—with his death. His loss. Whatever the hell it was.

He was gone and I was never going to see him, and the fact that the man I knew was gone even before I saw him fly off that thousand foot cliff—no longer my brother—somehow assaulted me more egregiously than anything else.

I missed him. Three simple, cliché words. But there was no better way to sum it up.

Granger brought the Frisbee back after snagging it airborne, panting and showing me her happy, smiley face. It made me feel better. Her perpetual happiness at everything always restored and reenergized me. I mistrusted people who didn't like dogs. Canines were just so absolutely loyal and loving and unconditional. They were far better "humans" than we were.

Allergies aside, if you didn't appreciate the dog, I was pretty sure I'd have a hard time appreciating you. That was just the way it was. That was why I always gave Jax so much shit about his alpacas. At least he had some working dogs to keep the wannabe llamas in line. But he didn't appreciate their hard work or loyalty. He didn't love them.

But I didn't hold it too much against him. As I said, he was my brother. For real. Yes, all cops (male and female) were my brothers. I had friends that treated me *better* than did my own blood. Still, nothing could change the fact that I'd have done anything for Jax.

I'd have damn well gone over that cliff edge in his place.

5

SPENCE FELT the plans were right on schedule, or the thing Spencer Grant had become—it had never been as if he were a single entity; he was the embodiment of who he had always been and who he was now capable of being with the passenger that rode forever inside him, whispering to him at times, howling in rage at others. It had been years since he knew the difference between the two Spences.

It didn't help that he looked nothing as his former self then. On the outside, those first few months in Denver, the thing inside him had changed his appearance so many times that he was forced into wonderment each new day as to who he might see in the mirror looking back at him. He always looked the very definition of "average" or "nondescript", though the thing inside was so evil Spence was sure it could have made him so ugly he'd have made newborn babies screech in horror.

No, the thing knew the plan; the thing was *in charge* and had been since the days in Idaho. Since he'd murdered his family. And once they were hiding in Denver—not just hiding, but holding out for more than *ten years*, Spencer Grant needed to never look the same twice.

After five years, his exterior was changed permanently. Or until the next time the beast inside wished him to look different, he supposed. But in any case, he no longer physically resembled his former self and hadn't for such a very long time. So much so that Detective Bobby Macaulay and Manny Rodriguez stood next to him in the store, and thanks to Bluetooth technology, were carrying on a conversation with him as he stood near a bus stop, just out of earshot.

Ten years. They'd waited *so long* and he'd killed *so many.*

The "famous crimes" posing was his idea. In his previous life, with the wife and children, he'd loved true crime television. He knew all there was to know about all the famous killings. This way he felt involved. The plan had nothing to do with the way the bodies were placed and the thing inside no doubt felt Spence's little improvisation was acceptable as it would keep the police on their toes, turned the wrong way (or thinking the wrong way when they were turned the right way, as that day at the 7-11).

The beast within was not pleased with Spence for that arrogant move. The call was preordained, but not the proximity from which Spence made it. It was a delicate relationship, that between him and the thing inside him. It wasn't that he ever really felt like the old Spence, but he felt at least *human* much of the time.

The thing inside, when it appeared physically, was humanoid in form but emanated such evil that Spence could not bear to look upon it. It didn't reveal itself to him often and for that he was beyond grateful. It was indescribably horrifying when it appeared, probably in part because it usually only appeared when Spence had made a mistake that required a reminder—an aide-mémoire of what LIVED inside him.

Also a gauche reminder of who ran the show.

What Spence had begun to call "the humanoid" for lack of a better name for the physical manifestation of his inner demon, appeared after the 7-11 incident and the phone call.

Spence was watching television in the upper level of the warehouse he'd converted to a dungeon and execution chamber under and behind the façade of a business he called Alberta Shipping. All the papers were in place for

Alberta; Spence had filing cabinets full of falsified shipping records. The office was next door to the small apartment-sized area Spence called "home". The horror all happened below.

"You were a stupid, stupid human today," the beast said to him, its voice crackly and throaty. Like it needed a perpetual clearing. The very sound of the thing almost made Spence piss himself, both because of its horrifying nature but, too, because there was never a precursor; nothing to warn Spence that dad was coming to punish his little boy.

And it was just as mortifying, even now after hearing it a hundred times.

"I'm sorry," Spence whispered, praying that his inner demon would not require his full visual attention. He didn't want to see it; didn't *need* to. The voice alone—the thing's declaration—was more than enough to teach him that his behavior was selfish and stupid.

"Turn and witness me when I address you. Remind yourself of who I am and that I am now a part of you."

Spence began to whimper. "I swear, it won't ever—"

"Turn. Around."

It wasn't exactly that it was different every time, though in a metaphysical way, it was. Each time it appeared was somehow magnitudes worse than the last, even though the humanoid shape and exterior looked like a newborn body covered in clear, dripping honey, the force that derived from inside the thing and filled the room was not something a human being was capable of comprehending and thus played horrible games with the mind.

Evil was unimaginable as pure embodiment. Those who'd never actually seen it—and there were so few who had—could not possibly imagine the raw, unbridled terror it caused the very soul of a human to look onto its formation. To sense of what it was capable; to *feel* what could only be described as hatred of Good, and of humans, and of anything normal—it was quite literally demonstrative to the spirit and capable of causing permanent scarring that could not be driven away by a stadium full of psychiatrists.

Spence slowly turned to the side, where he knew the creature had chosen to appear. The smell had hit him already and thankfully he'd grown accustomed to the stench—that, at least, was a tangible. As detectives and police became accustomed to decomposition or meat factory workers to opened flesh, Spence had become desensitized. It was the only reason he did not vomit as he had the first dozen or so times. The most fear came in the moment *before* he looked upon his demon. The anticipation.

When he looked, mercifully, the horror was so overwhelming he immediately lost control of all bodily functions and collapsed unconscious.

He awoke hours later in pools of his own excretions. It was nauseating, but the fear of what he'd experienced in his mind and soul before passing out was far more damaging than the smell of anything *human*, excrement or not.

Spence checked the day and the time. He had no idea how long he was out, but the freshness of the mess in which he rested suggested it had not been too long. It was four in the morning. Mac wasn't due a call for his next surprise until the next day. The thing wanted *MacAulay*, as it referred to him, emphasizing verbally the traditional spelling, to know he was always a step behind. Cat and mouse. More than once Spence wondered what Mac's family had done to so enrage the Evil of the world.

Truthfully, he didn't want to know.

He decided instead of such contemplations he would clean himself and his apartment.

"Manny, I had an important realization yesterday."

"Good to see you again, boss," Manny told me.

"Run a profile on Melissa Grant, from Rocky Gap, Idaho. I want to know everything the system has on her. Also call the police up there, the new Chief, uh, Brown. Jeffers Brown. Get everything they have, too. I mean BOLOs, everything."

"Done."

"We need her birthdate first," I said.

"Give me a minute," Manny said, and spun in his chair. "I can get that for you in a shake."

Technology. I loved it. God it made the cop's job easier.

"September twentieth," Manny said two or three minutes later.

"She'll be nineteen," I said.

"What?"

"Nineteen. In a month. We've got one month to get to Spence Grant or his daughter will die."

"Mac, we don't even know if she's alive. He could have let her go. More likely—and I hate saying this, partner—but he probably killed her before scooting out of

Idaho. Buried her in the wilderness, bones now picked clean."

"He told me he brought her with him."

"He could have lied. Probably lied. No matter how much he disguised himself, no matter how many times, do you know how much harder it would be to live in a city on the lookout for the child that was with you—for a month, much less for *ten years?*"

"I know. I know what the books and the procedures and the odds say. But I think I may have figured a pattern that relates to the number nineteen. The victims' ages. They're not random. This is another of his crazy games. Running the rat through the maze."

"Who's *he?* You're sounding kind of paranoid, partner."

"How many victims?" I said.

"Hailey Carpenter made nine," Manny answered with that young man, everything-was-a-bet-or-competition swagger.

"Your confidence betrays you," I said.

"Meaning?"

"You're thinking *nine bodies plus one, Melissa Grant, does not equal nineteen.* That we've got nine more bodies coming for Melissa Grant to make number nineteen on her nineteenth birthday—which there's not time for based on the length of time in the killer's M.O.—so there's no way my 'nineteen being special' theory is correct."

"Okay, well, yeah, I *was* thinking something along those lines. It's the detective in me, boss. Sorry."

I loved that kid. He had all the makings of a *great* detective. Better than me. He was still too young for me to say so, because it would ruin him. I was grooming him like a racehorse. Slowly. Giving him his confidence a day at a time. No rushing a work of art, and I wanted Manny to be my legacy in the department.

I hadn't told him about my thoughts of retirement. Thing was, I could not leave until Manny Rodriquez was as good as I could make him. I figured a year, two tops. Then I could retire and give back to my wife what I had selfishly taken from her: chasing the bad guys.

I could do that for her.

But not until Detective Manolo Rodriguez was ready.

"You much of a math guy in school?" I said.

"Fucking hated it."

I hated *that*. Manny wasn't much of a curser when I met him. He'd picked up on my favoring of the F-word. Kids did the same thing with their parents. I personally didn't think a word was anything but an emphasizer or a punctuation mark but a lot of folks take umbrage with profanity and I knew I was the one who instilled that in him.

I also knew, like kids, he'd have picked it up anyway. Every cop I knew cussed like a made Mafioso, man and woman. It was a matter of time; I just didn't relish being his mentor in that regard.

"Grab the ages of our victims and I am going to do a small but significant math trick for you," I said.

Manny grabbed the file and I got up and cleaned a space on our whiteboard.

"Read the victim ages, in order," I told him.

"16, 22, 19, 20, 19, 20, 19, 17, 19."

"Remember the terms mean, median, and mode?"

"From math," he said.

"From math."

"Vaguely."

"Well you're not alone. Don't feel bad, it was a hunch but I had to look them up on the Internet last night to make sure I had them right."

Manny's face de-scrunched and the slight frown that had formed went flat. The competition in that kid—

"Mean is simple. It's the average; average and mean, same thing."

"So you total and divide by the number of numbers," Manny said proudly.

"Yep."

"Let me guess, nineteen is the avera—I mean, mean. Shit, that's a double untundra or something."

"Uh, double entendre, and no, it isn't—that would take you into English class."

"Oh, I hated English more than Math. You gringos have the most fucked up language I know."

"Fair enough, but you got it right, nineteen is the mean."

"What're the other two?" Manny was literally like a kid in school now.

"Median is the number in the middle. So if you look at the listing of the ages of our victims…"

"Nineteen, smack in the middle."

"Yes, again, grasshopper."

"What the fuck is that supposed to mean?"

"Young Jedi?"

"Ahh, right. Okay, still don't know what a grasshopper has to do with any of this, but gotcha."

"Mode," I said, "is the number in the sequence used most often."

"Nine-fucking-teen," he said.

"Watch the language. Yoda would shove his walking stick up your ass, young Rican Jedi."

"I like that—call Lucas; the next Jedi needs to be a fucking 'Rican."

"So are you with me on this nineteen thing or do I have to sell it to the lieutenant on my own?"

Manny scowled again.

"What's up," I asked.

"I got your back no matter what."

I'd have this young man ready in less than a year. Hell, maybe six months. In less than a year the love of my life could have her old job back. I had no idea what the fuck *I* was going to do.

"Hey, Jedi," I said.

"Yeah, boss?"

"We'll work the angle of his daughter being next. But we'll watch for more victims. Keep the undercover women out on the streets. No reduction in force. We're covering every base on this one."

It was *after* we were seated in Lieutenant Elias Shackleford's office that I realized I'd not yet sprung the "Spencer Grant" appearance on him either, as I had promised to do with all bravado in front of my partner. Well, might as well put my young partner's "got your back" creed to the test.

"What do you have?" Shackleford asked and began moving things around on his desk. The lieutenant was easily the neatest man I'd ever known and the few objects on his desk—a picture of his wife and children, a golf bag pen-holder, a Post-it container, and an obsidian paperweight—had never changed position or moved at all as long as he'd been my boss. But he moved them out of position and back like a three card monte dealer with OCD. Still, any lack of eye contact with Elias Shackleford was a small blessing.

"I have a theory, L-T," I said. "Actually, I received a rather, uh, let's refer to it as strange and fortuitous phone call the other day."

"Mmm-hmm," Shackleford mumbled.

"The caller was Spencer Grant."

The lieutenant froze. He peered up. He didn't seem pleased (although I am not sure what 'pleased' looked like on my boss). "You're telling me the caller *claimed* to be Grant?"

"I am telling you it was him. I know his voice."

"Trace on the phone that called you?"

"A burner. In fact, we were *at* 7-11 getting tape—I mean capture—from the security camera there because we were lucky to track down the purchase location of the cell that called our pizza delivery guy to the Hailey Carpenter scene."

"So he was following you. Or knew you'd trace the phone—or both," Shackleford said.

"Likely a yes to all," I said. "Manny was able to put a pretty good match in build to Grant entering the 7-11, buying a batch of phones, and leaving. He had a hoodie hiding his face, but I know it was him."

"How so?" Shackleford said.

"He waved at the closest camera as he walked by," Manny said.

"Probably doesn't want to give away his disguise," I said.

"Any of the other burners been used?"

"No," Manny said.

"What else. You said 'theory', Mac, not perp identification."

Oh, boy. This was where the road split and I was afraid of the path less-traveled.

"Were you a big math guy, sir?"

"Come again?"

"Look, I am going to cut to the chase. You will or won't like it: the mean average, median, and mode of our victims' ages is nineteen."

"Interesting," Shackleford said, intertwining his long fingers and looking speculative. "Mean and average are repetitive, though. Same thing."

"Yes, sir. I'm aware."

Then, out of left field, from the cheap seats, a hundred mile an hour spit ball:

"Good detective work, Mac. This is the kind of strange shit that solves cases."

For the moment, I was stunned into silence.

"There's more," I said, glancing at Manny, a bit confused.

"September twentieth is Melissa Grant's nineteenth birthday," said the boss.

"Yes," I said.

"Which means his daughter *is* with him in Denver and it's likely we have a month to find this psychotic bastard."

"That's the best—our best—theory, Lieutenant." I said.

"I concur. But stay alert, men. There are still a lot of days for this turd to chalk up another nine killed and make his own daughter number nineteen."

"Agreed," I said.

Manny nodded, and we left.

"There's more," I whispered as we returned to our freshly installed, seven-foot cubicle walls. Manny waited until we were seated and gave me his undivided attention. "This story I need to tell you should be done somewhere other than here."

"What about *Deb's?*"

"Too many cops. We need to talk openly. You're also probably going to need a drink or two for this and we're on duty."

"I know a 'Rican spot that's perfect. Well, I wouldn't send you down there alone, but with me, you are *en buenas manos*. Safe in my hands, partner."

I let Manny drive and he took us into a neighborhood I'd never been in before. Clearly Puerto Rican. Once we got there, Manny's body stance and language shifted slightly. The homeboy had gotten out, but was still a homeboy nonetheless. I had never felt before that my life was in my partner's hands as much as that moment. Alone, I'd have never made it back to familiar streets unharmed, of that I was sure. But I trusted Manny.

He slipped into an alleyway and then quickly pulled the Charger left and into a gravel spot with no markings and the smell of sweet cooking pork in the air.

"Back entrance," Manny said, swaggering.

'Rican.

I nodded, feeling that white-and-way-the-hell-outta-place thing. Almost like my whole body had swelled and made me look gargantuan and on display.

We entered a dark room, made significantly worse by our sun blindness. As my eyes adjusted I realized the place was maybe half the size of our small squad room.

Manny went straight for a booth and lifted his head to the brown-skinned, waifish girl behind the bar who returned the gesture. She appeared at our table with two sweating bottles of *Dos Equis* ambers.

"Gracias, mija," Manny said, showing those *love ya* teeth.

"De nada, Manolo. Hola, Mac."

My surprise was evident.

"Manny, he talk about you. Good stuff. Good man. You're welcome here any time, sexissimo." And the gorgeously plain bartender spun and disappeared to a room behind the bar.

"She likes you," Manny said.

"I got that with the sex thing."

"*Sexissimo*. It's slang, not very 'Rican, actually. And usually it's *sexissima* and catcalled at the ladies."

"Still a compliment, I'll assume," I said and took a pull on the *Dos Equis*. It was delicious.

"She meant it nice. And she meant you could come anytime and feel safe. Adelmira has pull in the 'hood. Daughter of a big guy, probably should stay nameless for now. Her name basically means 'from nobility'. By the time we get back to the station everyone around here will know you're *intangible*. Untouchable. It's why I brought you here."

"Where is 'here'?"

"Mira's Place."

"Original name."

"Puerto Ricans get to the point." He took a drink.

"We're not going back to the station," I said. Manny nodded and signaled to Adelmira for another pair.

"This story—this, *history*—few know it."

A nod.

"My wife. Me. Spence Grant. That's about it. Bum Garvey I told recently."

"Glad you threw Amanda and Bum in there. They'll bring the story that touch of acceptability, I hope."

"Trust me, if it were just me and Spence Grant I'd have checked *myself* in."

"Wow. We're definitely not going back to the house."

"Not likely," I said. Adelmira returned with two fresh beers and two shots of clear tequila.

"Patron Silver. You both have that look about you. So serious. Lighten up; 'He enjoys true leisure who has time to improve his soul's estate.' Thoreau."

"Gracias, Adelmira. For everything," I said. My Spanish was bad; I tried nothing more intricate than a thank you.

"Mira to you, Bobby Mac. And you are most welcome."

Manny picked up his shot glass, raised it toward me, and downed it. I followed suit. Mira smiled and left.

"It's not our custom to wait. Direct. Remember that," Manny said.

"*Excelente*," I said, pointing to the empty shot glass. "Time for a tall tale, I'd say."

"Speak. And hesitate not."

I started at the beginning, which was not a cliché because I had thought long and hard about how much to tell him, which parts, what order. In the end, the truth might actually set me free. So I started at the beginning.

I told him about the MacAulay history, the Book of Ossian, Father Fic Rule, the demons—all of it. I even told him about Amber. How it *was* self-defense but that she was not herself, she was possessed of the demon Rule. Or Satan himself.

We drank as I talked. More tequila. More *Dos Equis*. And Mira never came close, never listened in, and no other patrons so much as looked in our direction. I watched Manny's eyes the whole time. I wanted to read him, know how he was taking this absolutely insane tale, what he was thinking—mostly what his impressions would now be of me.

Finally I told him about the mountaintop, and about Jax. How he died; what Rule *did to him* before he died.

And then I was done. Two hours. Four. I really couldn't have guessed how long the story took. We sat in silence after I finished. Manny sipped on his beer and I signaled my new favorite Puerto Rican bartender for another round of Patron.

"*Madre de Dios*," Manny said, and crossed himself.

I had no idea he was even religious.

6

THE CALL came in just after the morning shift had started the next day. A female uniform had run down from the eighth floor to speak to me in person.

"Detective Macaulay," she shouted. I stood in my cubicle and waved her over. "Officer Freitas, sir. A phone call came in, from Special Tactics. Hostage situation and the taker is asking for you personally."

This couldn't be happening again. That was my first thought. Then, *why fight it?*

"Location?"

"Overpass at Evans and I-25. They've stopped all traffic on the freeway and on Evans in both directions. It's a school bus, Detective. He's driven it through the barrier and it's hanging forty-five feet in the air. He's threatening to drive it the rest of the way over the ledge if you aren't there in twenty minutes."

"Come on," I said to Manny as I ran from the cube. "Did he give a name at least?"

"The man said to tell you his name is Rule."

The scene was as described. The bus—a smaller version of a regular bus with a handicapped symbol on the sides and back—had indeed been driven through the concrete barrier and was teetering on the edge.

"What in fuck's sake is up with you, Macaulay?" Len Brighton said to me for the second time in as many months. "You should join up with us."

He handed me the cell phone and I slowly placed it against my ear.

"Bobeeeee."

"Good Christ, Grant, what the hell are you doing now?"

"Good one with the 'Rule' bit, eh? Bet that got the old heart pumping."

"Come on, Grant. Let's talk this through—"

"Bad tactics, Detective. Negotiations one-oh-one. Befriend the taker. I've asked you *at least* a half dozen times to call me Spence."

"Okay, Spence."

"And never, ever sound defeated, Mac. You never want your own stress or emotions to transfer to the taker. Think what it might make him do."

"Do you have any demands?" I just couldn't take this joker any longer. It was like a bad episode of Batman. "Or are we just gaming here, Spence?"

"I never actually thought that far ahead," he told me. "Shit. World peace, I guess. And let Charlie Manson go, too. That old fart couldn't harm a fly he's so bat-shit crazy."

"This is serious, Spence. You've got school children on board."

"Special needs."

"What?" I said.

"These are all special needs kids, Mac. You know, short bus and all."

Oh, God. I hadn't even let the logic open up my brain.

"Shit, Spence—"

"There's that deflated sound again," he said. "And swearing? Never, ever swear at the taker. He might get offended."

I didn't want to talk to him anymore. I wanted to give the phone to Brighton and go home. Retire *today*. It wasn't a brave or courageous thought. But it was what I wanted. I couldn't stop thinking about the tropical pictures on the computer that Amanda sent me. I happened to look over at my partner—at Manny. The look on his face was like a punch to my solar plexus. The disappointment. The pleading in his eyes for me to do something. His father figure. His hero. I went back to the phone.

"Let's quit gaming, Spence, what do you say? Let's figure out what you're planning here because we both know you're not here for demands."

"Oh but I *am*, Mac. You know those ice cream trucks? The ones that drive around the neighborhoods playing that god-awful music that drives me nuts all summer day long?"

"Yes."

"I want eight cones from one of those trucks. No, make it eight of the orange popsicles, what do they call 'em? Creamsicles. Orange on the outside, vanilla cream in the center. The ones you used to beg your parents for when the truck came 'round during Gilligan's Island."

"What the f—how could you know that?"

"Come on, Mac, we're waaaaaay past those kinds of questions, now aren't we?"

"Eight?" I said.

"Come back?"

"You said you needed eight? You have eight hostages?"

"Nine, Mac. Nine. You know this part. Eight kids and one bus driver. But just bring eight because Wanda here looks like she needs one of those Slim Fast bars. You know what? Round her up one of those while you're getting ice cream for the retards."

He almost got me with that one. I nearly tossed the phone and rushed the bus.

"You loved the math puzzle, didn't you?" Spence said. "You and that aptitude test when you were, what, six? Seven?"

"Let's talk about the kids, Spence. Okay?"

"You were high in all the areas, but off the charts in verbal and math. A real honest-to-god *genius*. And what'd your dad do with the test results?"

"The kids, Spence. Don't hurt the kids."

"Good old Paddy. He took one look at those outstanding scores and he crumpled them up and tossed them in the old fireplace, now didn't he?"

"Paddy was a hero."

"Because he was a fireman? Is that why, Mac? Or is it because of that good old Scottish temper?"

"Shut up, Grant."

"You didn't mind taking a beating. But when he went after Jackson, that really got to you, didn't it?"

"Grant, I swear to Christ—"

The cops had all gathered around me by now. I was at the edge of meltdown. Red in the face. Sweat running as through a sieve. Trembling. I couldn't imagine what my eyes must've been saying. I knew what I was thinking:

I didn't care. I didn't care what happened to any of them, as long as I got my hand around that son-of-a-bitch's neck. It was past all rules and regulations. They didn't make 'em for this type of onslaught anyway. And I knew those poor children and their terrified bus driver didn't stand a chance anyway.

"Here's the real mathematical beauty of it," Spence whispered into the phone. "When you do all the ages, along with this old bus driver, you're going to come up with the same number."

The bus engine roared to life and the back wheels started burning rubber and before any of us could think, much less react, the bus went front-first over the edge, as in slow motion, and landed on its top, its own weight and the force of gravity crushing everything and everyone inside on the freeway pavement below.

Shackleford called a meeting of the entire squad. He wanted to examine the procedures of the bus scene, identify mistakes, and learn as a team, in the open. It was his protocol but this wasn't a homicide case, not technically. Our jobs began AFTER the victims were killed.

Which was why the bulk of his remarks and inquisition were directed at me.

"When a busload of innocent children—special needs kids, no less—goes down on our watch—and by 'our watch' I mean the Denver Police Department as a whole as well as members of this unit on scene—the public wants answers and they want them now."

In the silence he looked at me, as if waiting for me to explain away what happened. I said nothing.

"When the public and the media demand answers, the Brass demands answers, and that makes the job of Lieutenant 'answer man'—and you know what? You take the shitty parts of the sandwich right along with the good fixings; that's what my father taught me."

Shackleford's dad retired as a Captain after twenty-five years. He'd also taught his son that twenty years was the MINIMUM for retirement and you never aim for the minimum unless it was a kill shot.

"May I say something," I asked.

"I was hoping we'd hear from you on this one, Detective. Seeing how your presence was requested yet again."

"First, it was a hostage situation. I—Detective Rodriguez and I—were there as requested but neither of us are recently trained in hostage negotiation."

"Noted," the boss said.

"Regardless, I think everyone in this room knows Grant intended to drive that bus over the edge no matter what was said or done."

"We can't know that and we certainly can't make that my official answer to One PP."

"No, we can't. But this is OUR meeting and I think facts as well as gut beliefs are relevant to how we perform our jobs," I said.

"You just might make a decent lieutenant one day, Mac," Shackleford said, released a breath, and sat down at the head of the table.

At least he'd lightened up, which meant my statement had served its purpose.

"The little boy. He's still alive?" the boss said.

I nodded. "He's nowhere near 'out of the woods', but he's alive," I said.

We'd found one autistic boy, nine years old, breathing. He'd crawled beneath a seat and the extra space—just a few inches—saved his life. The only survivor. We announced officially to the press that all were believed to have perished, hoping to delay the facts a day or two at most. We did, of course, notify the family immediately and prior to any statements that their son had so far survived but to not speak to anyone about those specifics yet.

"The suspect was not found in the wreckage?"

"No, sir. We believe he was never on the bus. Our working theory is the driver was in on the plan. Or forced to do what she did."

"To drive herself and eight handicapped children to their deaths?"

"Yes."

It sounded preposterous, but we took apart the bus, even looking for escape hatches, hidden compartments—it was a compacted mess. I even consulted a magician whose specialty was in the area of "escape artist". I brought him in to examine the evidence, hear the story, watch the news footage of the bus from all angles based on the fact that media helicopters were on the scene and filmed the entire incident.

He said, and I quote:

"If a man was on that bus, he made the greatest escape of all time."

Spence Grant was never there. No one could say they'd actually seen him firsthand. He claimed he was calling from inside the bus, but he could have been anywhere. The news footage did not show the inside of the bus; windows and doors were closed and the Colorado sunshine hid the interior as well as if the windows had been tinted.

Shackleford and the rest could clearly not imagine how the bus driver—a woman driving for the school district for twenty-seven years, no police record, no traffic stops, and a devout Mormon, could have been convinced to carry out such a horrific act.

But I knew.

And now so did Manny.

If he believed it.

7

I STOOD in the JDK3 Task Force war room. It was still a couple of hours before the rest of the team would arrive and the day begin. We all had our "day jobs", though we worked them as second priority and in the off hours. It was quite the orchestration, bringing so many law enforcement personnel from myriad agencies, departments, and jurisdictions together for just *one* meeting, much less three to five a week, depending on developments. And we'd most certainly had a "development" with the appearance of Spence Grant after all these years. It was my briefing this morning and all I could think about was how much or how little to tell.

Not unlike the forever battle in my mind—or rather, between my mind and soul—my mind being the source of reason and logic and the known world; the things we can touch and smell and taste; the things that made the world what it was to us, made some kind of reason out of a predicament the human race had really never fully understood.

The soul, of course, being the source of love and dreams and, in many cases, beliefs, even when the mind and the ways of our known universe implied otherwise. I remembered something Father West—my cousin; a Macaulay—told me years ago when I was struggling mightily to grasp the meaning of what we'd seen, done, been witness to—and let me be clear about something: seeing a thing and being witness to it were two entirely separate things and not open to semantic interpretation. Seeing is a physical act; we observe the thing—the happening—and perhaps, depending on various elements such as the level of shock, vantage point, and yes, even belief system, we retain, at some basal level, a recording or remembrance of the circumstance.

Witnessing an event implies something much deeper and completely different. Witnessing does not happen with the eyes; it is not a physical thing but a metaphysical or, if you prefer, a spiritual one. It occurs within the realm of ourselves that we refer to as a soul, an un-seeable, untouchable, un-examinable (at least with modern instruments) organ but nonetheless the most palpable one we have as sentient human beings. We do not weigh it—cannot—but it weighs us.

Manny was the most recent to hear my story. I'd only ever shared it with a handful of people, most of them—scratch that, all—because they had to know; because whatever moment of a case or an investigation or, most important of all, the saving of lives, depended on them hearing it. After hearing it rather than seeing it firsthand, they and they only were capable of bearing witness and measuring, searching inside, grappling with the inconceivable, and coming out the other side with a personal level of belief and understanding on their own.

I was always careful to make clear we were not talking about anything that had not been part of human history as long as it had been recorded; I was not speaking of witches, warlocks, werewolves, vampires, ghouls, ghosts, or zombies. I headed off the natural reaction of dismissing the telling as if a ghost story. I believed the mind's reaction to the telling craved a way to somehow de-legitimize the reality of what was being shared.

For millennia the story—my story—had been told, and not in fairytale books or around campfires but in churches and synagogues and temples all around the world by every cogent religion since nearly the beginning of time.

God and the Devil.

Good versus Evil.

A great preponderance of people on the planet would not call these things paranormal—beyond the normal—at all. In fact they would argue emphatically that these "stories" were not the background noise of the universe but the very stage upon which humanity played out its meek and unfinished existence; a play with (at least for us) an unknown ending.

And was it so hard to believe that I was part of a lineage whose sacred duty had been—for hundreds, perhaps thousands of years—tasked with waging a battle on the side of Good; a war against the sometimes unbelievable and inexplicable elements of Evil?

It was for me. I was a detective, first and foremost. Our entire process depended on empirical evidence. The touchable. The seeable. The tangible. *Evidence.*

Then again, any good cop would tell you that half of what he or she did—particularly the successful half—was due to intuition. Call it what you would: gut feeling, instinct, intuition, hairs standing at attention on the arms and necks, goose pimples, little devils and angels on the shoulder.

The *para*normal. Beyond physical or instrumental explanation. But there wasn't a decent investigator alive or dead that would tell you, if they could, that such un-seeable, un-measurable, unsubstantiated elements were not only key to solving cases but perhaps central and most important of all.

I stared at the evidence board—the summation of all we'd seen, done, found, and yes, witnessed (although I might be the only one in the room, other than my best friend, who believed we'd witnessed anything at all— particularly by my definitions).

So many young women—girls, most. Underage by every definition of the word. So brutally their lives were snuffed from existence. Did they believe it in the end—what they'd *witnessed?* Did they believe in the existential reality of Good and Evil—God and the Devil? Had they seen the demons as I had?

The irony was that we humans use the term all the time. Battling our demons. The return of our demons. The word was practically universally codified in the handbooks for addicts all over the planet.

But to tell—to even imply—one had seen a demon, much less a horde of them? Well, at that point we were normally talking white coat time. Psych lockup. As if we humans had it all figured out. We'd been here on this planet for perhaps a fraction of an eye blink next to the age of the Universe itself yet we were arrogant enough to think we knew all the answers.

Never mind that those "answers" changed almost daily; never mind that what we knew yesteryear (the Earth was flat; we were the center of the universe; there was no cure for Polio; there were x number of planets in this solar system or that); never mind the theories (and discoveries) of wormholes and Quantum Physics and the fact that science itself—the most elephantine skeptic in the room—literally thrived on the next *unknown* discovery around the corner.

Since the beginning of the killings and my participation in their investigation I had felt the palpability of my involvement. Not physically on the team or even my selection to it. That was logical. No, I had sensed more. A lot more. Yes, I had missed the Spence Grant connection but, A) That was more than likely as preordained as it was poor detective work; and, B) It really didn't change much in terms of the why, where, and when for the next victim.

It gave us a name. Perhaps another path; another starting point into an abyss of the unknown. But it did not give us any of the answers for which we searched. However, it pulled on me—it had my insides firing on every piston. I was excited; I felt as if I was but an inch from knowing the why, where, when and from catching that son of a bitch.

But then I also knew that finding him—discovering the "master plan"—was in all likelihood only the beginning. "Beginning" being as stretching and warming up was to the "beginning" of the twenty-six mile run, one-mile swim, and one hundred mile bike ride of an Iron Man Triathlon.

Yet I needed desperately to cover that last inch so that we could finally, after all these months and all these deaths, truly begin the race.

I was still staring at the pictures on our investigation board when Bum Garvey walked into the room, himself still over an hour early for the meeting.

"Figurin' on changing anything by starin' long enough at them pictures or were you just tryin' to divine some new leads through some kind of Jedi mind meld?"

I smiled and shook my head slowly. Bum always made me feel better. He was the Hardy to my Laurel; a great man who had been in service to his country since I was learning to watch Dick run and Spot take a dump. "It's just all so overwhelming," I said.

"That it is," he said. "But that's not why you are here hours before the sun is up and with a look of worry on that face that could discourage the Dali Lama himself."

"There are new developments," I told him. "The problem is, with these developments comes a lot of baggage. And not the kind that's easy to explain or defend."

"Last I looked, the charter of this team was to find the killer, not explain or defend how we do it."

"You're right. But these developments—these people and the elemental beliefs that fall into question when discussing them—well, it is never easy to talk law enforcement personnel into much that falls outside the empirical, if you know what I mean."

"Devils and demons and such?" Garvey said.

"Among other things."

"You know why you were picked for this unit, right?" Garvey said, standing up to walk toward starting the coffee pot in the corner. "I mean beyond being one of the goddamned finest detectives I've ever known."

"Guess I thought that was why."

"You ever been on one of these task forces before?"

"No," I said. "I never have."

"And suddenly you're on this one," Bum said. "Kinda begs a question or two, don't it?"

"What're you poking around at, Bum?"

"Stories fly around law enforcement circles faster'n anywhere I've ever seen," he said. "Some people wanted you on this team *because* of the developments, elements, whatever, of which you speak, partner."

"Some people?"

"Yep."

"Maybe just one?"

Garvey poured the water in the coffeemaker and looked up, his bushy moustache and leathered face as emotionless as paper, or air. "Maybe. What difference does it make? Here's what you do this day, Mac: you say what needs sayin'. You tell these people what happened. They're good people and good cops and not one of them didn't want you on this team. Not one. So they'll listen to ya, too. They will."

"Thanks, Bum."

"You can thank me down at the pub after you get your ass laughed outta this conference room."

"And you can remind me again why the hell I listen to you," I said.

"Because of my genius, good looks, and inestimable charm. Plus when I drink I end up buying all the rounds."

"Most truthful thing you've said today."

"They trust you, Mac. But you gotta *let* 'em."

8

I STOOD before the group of elite law enforcement personnel. The funny thing that hit me was that even police could be afflicted with "cop panic". I was intimidated as hell. But I tried to breathe steadily, concentrate, and remember Garvey's words.

"I think it's time we put a bullet in the elephant," I said.

Not so much as a chuckle. It was a tough crowd.

"You all know my story. I am not going to stand up here and tell it nor will I defend it. It is what it is and the only parts of it that matter are those that help us catch this fucking killer."

Graveyard silence.

"I don't know any of your religious beliefs," I said. "I don't care. I am most of the time confused about my own. But I know I am sane, I know what I have *witnessed*, and I know that there is more at play here than cops like you all and myself are used to dealing with on a daily basis. Beyond that, I'd rather this be more of a sharing of information through questions and answers. I'll tell you whatever you want to know. I'll tell you my working theories, crazy as they may sound. But I'm pretty sure each one of you has a shitload of questions for me so why don't we start there?"

Steve Jenkins, Deputy Director of the Colorado Bureau of Investigations, took the opportunity like a hungry lion spotting a fresh kill unattended.

"You think this is God and Devil and demon possession, don't you?"

Jenkins had no middle ground, no places in which he tiptoed.

"Sir, as you well know and with all due respect, nothing is as simple as that."

"But you *are* implying to us that there is something preternatural to these killings, are you not?"

"Yes," I said.

"I knew your old man, son," Jenkins said. "Paddy was a mean son of a bitch, but he was one of the most honest, worthy men I've ever had the pleasure to know. Whatever you've got to say, whatever you've seen or know, I am ready to hear it."

In the silence following the Deputy Director's statement you could've heard a gnat cough. Jenkins didn't get to where he was being anyone's pal, so I appreciated the vote of confidence even more.

"You've no doubt all heard a variation of the stories," I said. "Only believe the most unbelievable parts."

The ovoid faces around the table turned to one another in my peripheral vision, my own eyes never leaving Deputy Director Jenkins. He nodded in understanding.

"My theory is that the bus driver herself drove those children to their deaths—sorry, almost all," I said.

"You believe a devout Mormon killed seven children, intent on killing them all as well as herself?" said Janet Del Rio, a supervising Sergeant and Detective in the Douglas County Sheriff's Department.

"I don't believe she was herself when she did it," I said.

"What exactly does that mean?" said Del Rio.

"I believe she was possessed."

At that moment, you'd have been able to hear the gnat *blink*.

"Son, you're askin' a lot from these educated, experienced lawpersons. Maybe a little truthful sharing of what you've learned, seen, done—whatever the case, might be in order. No one is here to doubt, and there ain't no crazy thoughts or theories, not if one brings us closer to the killer, or killers. The only 'crazy' far as I'm concerned is out there murdering innocent young ladies," said Garvey. "And now children."

So I told them. I was so tired of holding it all in I told them everything. Except the part about Greer. That one stayed within my circle of trusted friends and family. No one else need hear of the worst night of my life. It bore nothing on the case at hand.

When I was through there were no immediate questions. I believed it was the shock. My own included. As I spoke, it hadn't sounded like me, or rather, it was as if I were listening to myself right along with the rest of the room.

"I think we've had enough for the morning," Jenkins said, popping the silence as if it were a balloon of nothing at all. It was almost noon and we'd begun at seven. "I think it's fair enough to say that we should be working on the premise we have less than a month before Melissa Grant is likely to be killed. Until something else alters that theory, I thank Detective Macaulay for his candor—that couldn't have been easy, particularly considering the audience—and beliefs aside, this is what we're going on."

"I disagree," said Janet Del Rio. "I'm sorry, this is just asking too much. No disrespect, Detective Macaulay. We each respect your reputation."

"None taken," I said. "I've wondered more than twice myself."

"What about the dimes," asked Kent Reams, a young star Special Victims detective. "We never released the fact that we found the dimes on all the victims."

"Who are we going to get to admit that?" Del Rio said.

The speakerphone lying in the middle of the conference room table rang just as Del Rio finished her question. We all looked around as if someone had farted. I was standing nearest so I pushed the button.

"Hello?" I said

"Bobeeeeee."

I frowned.

"And everyone else, hello. It is 'who', Ms. Del Rio, to answer your question. Spence Grant. I am the one who's going to know about the dimes. Do you have any idea how hard it's been finding so many dimes minted before 1965? I should get some sort of award for that alone. Well, never overstay your welcome I always say. Oh, and don't worry Ms. Del Rio—I won't say a word to the team about the *other* Ms. Del Rio."

The phone and Janet Del Rio's complexion went dead.

Officer Rico came up to Homicide the day after I dropped my nuke on the task force. I really wasn't in the mood for an apology. Good thing. He didn't come toting one; he came to take me up on my offer of three rounds in the ring.

"Detective Macaulay," he said, him out of uniform, off duty, sweat-stained grays from wherever he worked out.

I looked up, my brain a million light-years away. "Uh, Rico. Yeah. What's up?"

"Figured you weren't going to call so since my Pilates place is just up the block decided I'd stop in so we could get that fight scheduled. The one where you're supposed to clean my clock or somethin' like that."

I leaned over my desk and motioned him in close so I could speak and not be heard by anyone but him. "Some friendly advice. No matter what your brain tells you to say, don't always say it. I am a Senior Detective and you are one year off boot status, so I say this not because I personally give a shit but because as you move along, your career's gonna care a lot. Step the fuck away from my desk now. You stink."

Rico stepped back. Said nothing, at least not with his mouth. His eyes wanted me in that ring right then.

"Guy down at the Third Precinct is a buddy of mine. Best ring in the city. I'll call and get us a couple hours, what, next Tuesday? You working nights still?" I said calmly.

"Yeah. I am still workin' nights. Sir."

"Today's Tuesday, right? What say you skip *Pilates* next week and we do this thing instead?" I looked up at the clock; I had no fucking idea what time it was. "Two to four PM?"

"See you there," Rico said, and spun to leave.

"Officer Rico," I said, loudly.

He stopped but didn't turn around.

"Bring plenty of ice."

I showed up at the Third Precinct gymnasium an hour early to get my sweat going. I was hoping no one had yet told the kid I was Golden Gloves five years running in my youth, half-Irish, and could have beaten most anyone in the DPD in their annual boxing championship tournament except I never entered for one reason: there was an undercover guy in Narcotics—grew up in Boston's Southie neighborhood—that just before joining the force was one bout from getting a shot at the World Welterweight Division Champion when he busted his hand on some brawler's thick skull in a charity fight. This guy fought every year—one of those ego guys—and he always won the trophy.

I had also never cozied up to the feeling of a fist hitting my face (gloves, head gear, or no). Not even when I was winning.

But this kid, Rico. I didn't want to fight him because of my ego or my anger or because of anything other than the brutal reality that being a cop was a dangerous gig and he had, hopefully, eighteen plus years ahead of him, and if he didn't take a beating now, he was going to die later.

At least that was what I told myself.

But I wasn't stupid. That Pilates shit; I knew the kid had the conditioning on me in a big way. I'd checked up on him and he'd done some boxing, half wins, half losses, dropped his gloves way too often, always looking for the big punches—I figured I had one round of beating on him, bruise him up good and sore, and then I just needed to wait for him to drop those gloves and knock him down and out near the beginning of the second round. If the fight went much longer than that, my gas tank would be running on fumes.

Rico didn't show up to the gym until fifteen minutes before, like he was suited up for a pick-up basketball game, no warm-up required for the old guy with one good leg. I was wearing what I referred to as my Pistorius—prosthetic strictly for athletics. It was actually even better for fighting than running, helping my bounce and weave.

By the time the bell rang for Round One, there were probably thirty other cops, mostly from Patrol, wanting to see their young stud champion stick it to the old man in Homicide. Score one for the grunts.

Rico danced around the ring like an idiot, kissing his gloves, throwing them to his buddies, acting like the ring rooster he was.

When he finally decided to stop showboating and fight, he came at me hard, just like I'd heard, young, dumb, and always looking for the knockout punch. He was five feet from our first contact when I changed my mind.

He dropped his gloves to cock that big right hook and I uppercut him so hard that his entire frame lifted a foot off the mat and when his legs came back down they may as well have been made of mashed potatoes.

Officer Rico crumpled like a shitty suit, right into the fetal position, and the ref didn't even bother counting. I walked back over to my corner, packed up my bag, and returned to make sure the kid wasn't dead.

He was just waking back up.

"You ever say anything to me about Burke, show any attitude to senior police, or I hear you're playing hot-shot quarterback out on the mean streets, we're coming back here and I am going to beat every square inch of pretty off that sexy face before lights out. You'll be so bruised and deformed the next shift they'll think you're the Elephant Man. Learn a lesson here. Be a good cop. I'm going to be checking up on you. You're my new favorite project."

I gave him the two fingers in the eyes "I'm watching you" sign. I guessed he was still seeing about eighteen fingers and I don't know how many sets of eyeballs. I looked at his partner—Gibbs, the guy who had his shit squared away—who was trying to get Rico to come around to his senses.

"You tell him," I said.

"Yes, sir."

He'd be all right. That was why I changed my plan, last second. Kid like that wasn't going to be humiliated taking a beating. His squad would probably start calling him Rocky or Balboa and he'd be hitting the streets every day thinking he could take on the whole wide world. What stung a guy like that—what taught Mr. Ego to wake up and smell the coffee beans—was being one hundred percent knocked the fuck out.

It doesn't get any more humbling in boxing than the one-punch down and out.

I wasn't even sweating anymore.

Somehow I knew Burke was looking down, laughing, and it made me want to sit down in the middle of the ring and cry.

Three nights earlier the humanoid had appeared for no reason—okay, Spence admitted to himself, no reason of which he himself was aware. It was changing, morphing, and if Spence wasn't bat-shit crazy, becoming even more human.

Yet it still held its control over him. That first night milling around the apartment, just to prove a point, the humanoid forced Spence into a twenty minute Irish jig. It sat in a chair in complete silence—expressionless—the entire time. There was no music, no happiness, no comedy—just Spence jigging around the open spaces in the apartment like a complete moron and the humanoid demon watching him.

When the thing relinquished control, it told him not to ever think for a moment that he was free of his bond with the creature, but that they'd entered a new stage of the grand plan—a plan to which Spence was most definitely *not* privy—and that the possessive occupation of Spence was no longer required.

Now, three nights later and a busload of children murdered, Spence wanted more than anything to garner a pat on the back or a "good work" or "well done."

"I did good, right?" Spence said to the creature.

The demon, of course, had no name, though as it changed, Spence knew exactly who the humanoid was. He'd not say it of course. Such a declaration would likely have him as dead as that fat bus driver and her gaggle of damaged children. Spence didn't care one way or the other who or what the humanoid would become nor what the master plan entailed, but the creature had been wandering around the warehouse, looking in on Melissa while she slept, which not only made Spencer sick to his stomach but also angry as hell—but what was he going to say?

"You did fine."

The creature spoke as if just recovering from a cold, phlegm and mucus still clinging to the insides of the throat. The eyes were striking. So blue they glinted like the sharpened edge of a surgeon's blade—and it was in those eyes Spence saw who it was. The thing's skin was beginning to form and it looked reptilian: cracked and broken. Like a kitchen tile smashed into a hundred pieces.

"Soon he'll know," the thing said.

"Macaulay?"

"The number. Judas, of course, as if a school child could not have figured that brainless clue. All of it. He knows it already, his subconscious simply won't let it loose inside his brain. The truth is too traumatic."

"Are you going to tell me what this all means?"

"Never."

"Won't I find out when your—when Macaulay figures it out?"

"If you're still alive to witness it."

Spence didn't say anything after that. He simply sat in the darkness and listened to the thing wheeze and gurgle and hate.

9

I FINALLY got a callback from Father Meyer West, my cousin, where he was volunteering in Cambodia alongside a congregation of Asian monks building homes made of the earth and bringing in fresh drinking water to the horde of homeless whose entire village had been decimated by a mudslide. I had sent multiple emails but heard nothing. There was no cell service in the remote area but he was able to call from a satellite phone that was slated for "emergency use only". According to him, the priests, nuns, and other volunteers used it when they became lonely and needed to hear a loved one's voice.

"Meyer?"

"Bobby. I can't believe it's you."

"We're in a bad way here in Denver," I said. "Serial killings, little girls. It's Spencer Grant."

"If Grant's involved, so is Father Rule," he said. "You realize this."

"I do realize it, although I'm not sure there's much of a distinction," I said.

"I don't know what I can do from here."

"When we were in Idaho you did a lot of research. You talked once of the real reason Rule could do what he does; why we'd not seen him before."

"You're breaking up," Meyer said. "Rule did what?"

"No, you said there was a reason he was here now."

"Not a reason," Meyer said. "A time. There's always been evil in the world, just as there's always been good. But that's the metaphysical; the intangible. Not devils walking the earth."

"But you thought you knew why it was real now. Physical demons and Rule and all of this other nonsensical shit. In the waking world with us."

"I said I had some thoughts on the subject."

"Well let's hear them. I am at the end of the killer's rope out here, Meyer."

"In the Book of Ossian there was foretold a betrayer in the Clan MacAulay. One who would not stand for Good but for the forces of Evil."

"And you were going to share this with me when?"

"Things have been so hard on you. I-I just didn't want to add more gloom where there was nothing to be gained. Even if it's accurate, it doesn't change much. I think we know enough to piece that part together."

"It still changes a lot, Meyer."

"Okay. Yes, I know. But that was my rationalization. The text was difficult to decipher at best, Bobby. You know that. The rest was more my supposition and intuition than printed in ink."

"I want to hear it anyway," I said. Meyer's lack of self-confidence could be trying at best.

"If a weak link in a chain weakens enough—"

"Broken chain," I said.

"The book also implied that somewhere around the fourteenth century the Clan was at its most powerful in both numbers and will and physical Evil was banished or put back somehow; back to whence it came."

"Hell?"

"Maybe, by one group's definition. A different place to someone else. We're way past the boundaries of any one or two religions, Bobby."

"So how can we find this rogue Macaulay?"

"I have no idea," Meyer said. "I told you, this is barely a pet theory."

"You're the smartest man I know," I said.

"No, Bobby. *You're* the smartest person you know."

"You know how much I hate that, Meyer."

"But sometimes you have to stop putting up the fight, cousin."

"If I'm so fucking smart, why can't I figure out a way to end this?"

"I'm betting the idea has already sprouted inside that thick skull of yours," Meyer said.

The ironic thing was, it had.

"I really feel in my being that you need to be here. Something beyond important is going down. That much I wouldn't hesitate to say, and I don't. We've won before but we've won together. There's significance in that, Meyer. Strength in numbers, power in blood."

"What I'm doing here, Mac. It fulfills me. Frankly, our previous encounters scared the shite right out of me. I'm not you, cousin. I'm an academic. A weakling. And a bit of a coward, I'm afraid."

"You are one of the bravest men I know, Meyer, and it's you alone who've taught me time and again that the mind is the strongest organ in the body. By *far*. I'm asking you to come."

"Then I will put aside my terror and find a way to be there for you, my cousin and friend," Father Meyer West said.

I had grown up despising my intellect. Could there be anything more egotistical than to think such a thing? It wasn't *my* label; I'd been labeled long before I had any memory of it. Two, three years old maybe. There were the tests and the examinations and, later, the special classes (those I *did* remember).

I wasn't exactly the nerd or the brain—I was tough and strong and an athlete, too, but Jax got to be the star and the ladies' man and the normal kid who got reprimanded by the teacher and, later, pummeled by our father for skipping class or pulling a "D" on a paper.

The dumb jock, he used to called himself, which was his way of joking to defend who he was against whatever jealousy or shortcomings or underachievement his ego claimed defined him. It was ridiculous. Jax was my best friend—not just a brother.

My best friend.

God how I missed him. I didn't know how or why or even when any longer that we'd allowed our differences to define and divide us, but we had. Our personalities were vastly different but much of that came from my own inability to put up with Jax's hatred of himself, his inability in his own eyes to live up to me, and the reality that there was no way for me to tell him that thoughts like that were bullshit or prove to him that I didn't feel that way or believe any of that at all.

I'd promised myself that when the shit was done in Idaho that we would talk—brother-to-brother, friend-to-friend, and figure everything out. Get back to where we used to be.

And then he was gone.

You spend a lifetime ignoring someone while they are but a phone call or an email away and then when they die you miss them every minute of every day. We couldn't connect to the afterlife, assuming there even was one.

It made no sense for me to disbelieve something after all I'd seen evidence of it, but I still had too much baggage to really accept all I'd been through. I wished my sharing of what I'd been told—what I'd witnessed—with the task force would have unburdened me somehow, but when I saw *that look* in their eyes, it was the same as back in the days of elementary school when the other kids realized I could read *Tom Sawyer* or *Ulysses* in the second grade.

The oddball.

The one who was different from the rest of them.

The child reading the classics, textbooks on Physics and Chemistry when he was ten.

Hell I couldn't just read them, I could recite them verbatim.

How was my brother ever supposed to compete with that?

My own father despised it. My abilities made my father feel like there was a superiority that came from my mother's side of the family, since all his kin had been laborers and blue-collar folk. So whom did he punish?

The son most like him.

Jax.

I could remember every blow, every whip of the belt, every slap.

And I could recall the agony in my brother's voice, right down to the decibel.

My own personal Hell.

A flawless memory.

Melissa Grant sat on her bed, ear buds in, listening to the Dropkick Murphys song *End of the Night* and wondered, not for the first time—not *nearly*—why she'd lived her life more as a prisoner than a daughter. Her father loved her, she knew that, but he could never come to explain the place they lived, where the rest of the family was—except to tell her they were patiently awaiting an arrival and that all these years it was she who was the most important piece in a thousand—even million—year struggle.

She sensed at times that her father was different now, but her memories of him *before*, well, they were too foggy most of the time—not unlike being in a dream state then waking and trying to remember the dream but literally watching it fade, second by second, in the mind.

Idaho she remembered.

That was the only memory that Melissa had that was strong. She could actually see the state's outline in her mind, the focus on the tallest top—the panhandle—where they used to live. Beyond that, not a lot. However there were memories there that, unlike her clouded memories of who her father used to be, felt blocked or locked away.

Memories of her mother and sister. They were more on the outreaches of her mind, constantly moving but finding all the doors and windows locked against them entering and Melissa, too, without the keys.

But Idaho was a place. At least she had that. Wherever she was now, there had to be a path toward Idaho. The world was finite. That meant there was nowhere from which she could *not* find a way home.

And she sensed that home was where the answers might be, or at least the beginning of the trail of breadcrumbs that would eventually lead her to the keys to unlocking her mind.

Which is why she decided that before her birthday she was going to run away. Or escape. Or whatever meant she didn't have to wonder any longer about the dark basement and the terrifying dreams of creatures visiting their home—a warehouse, she corrected herself, not even a home.

Idaho.

Home.

Family.

As the music washed over her she could think of nothing that would make her more whole again.

And if her father pursued? So much the better. Because she knew when he, too, saw *home*, he would remember the life they used to have, just as she would then be able to remember and embrace the same, and all would be okay again.

She'd formed a plan. Her father was not stupid. Far from it. And he watched her closely—not twenty minutes ago he'd rapped lightly on her door (she didn't hear him because of the ear buds and rocking Irish music, she simply knew his routines to the furthest degree necessary to complete her escape), opened it, and looked in on her. He didn't say anything or ask her to remove her music. He rarely said anything. It was more like a prison guard stopping by to make sure the inmate was still housed properly.

No conversation necessary.

He smiled benignly and half-waved.

Melissa smiled back then returned to playing an invisible set of drums.

After he closed the door she stopped the ridiculous air-drumming and lay still on her bed, thinking about her escape plan.

Melissa knew once she breached the outer perimeter of whatever place held her—a place she'd never been outside of—that she'd have minutes only. Maybe less. Even though she'd never seen the outside, she was intelligent enough (and had heard and seen enough) to know that her presence there was heavily secured, and she knew she would have to assume the worst: fences, motion detection, and cameras. All this meant that there was little to no chance of Melissa Grant exiting the warehouse and compound that likely surrounded it without detection.

Which was why she knew she'd only have minutes. And if she only had minutes, she'd need someone to come and get her.

So she calculated her best chance of making it home and that way was by finding a way to reach out. A few days earlier her father had brought home a bag of cell phones purchased at a convenience store. There were six or seven still in the plastic cases. And she'd seen a number under a name, scribbled on a scrap of paper on her father's desk. She'd committed the name and the number to memory, leaving the paper scrap untouched.

Macaulay.

720-555-3479

Melissa had no idea who Macaulay was, but it was her only hope. If he was a bad guy, her plan was over. If he didn't have a clue as to who she was or didn't want to get involved, her plan was over.

A trapped, starving mouse could not afford to ignore a scrap of cheese for fear of it being poisoned.

This was her one chance and she was going to take it.

Call this Macaulay, describe her imprisonment, ask for help.

She did not know how to tell him or her where she was. Her plan was to have this Macaulay on the phone as she escaped, calling out any landmarks, street names, corporate building names, signs—anything that might lead her rescuer to her.

It would have to be a race between her murderous father and this person, Macaulay, who though she did not know him or her, she hoped was the hero type.

Either way, whoever reached her first got the prize.

An almost nineteen-year-old, un-socialized recluse, scared shitless, nearly-clueless girl.

Quite a take.

I was on my way to a rare night out with my wife when my cell rang. When I looked down and saw it was *not* the job, and on top of that a number I did not recognize, I almost put the phone back in my pocket.

With triplets, Amanda and I hadn't had more than half a dozen private moments since their birth. We were both cops. Who would we trust with our little angels? As it happened, a year or so back Bum Garvey's daughter turned fifteen and decided to start a babysitting enterprise.

Thursday nights had since become "our" night. Zoë Garvey slated us for three hours every week and we either caught a movie or went to dinner, just the two of us. Sometimes, both.

The cop in me, however, wouldn't let the call go.

"Hello."

"Is this Macaulay?"

My insides turned to Jell-O. It was the voice of a teenager, but not Zoë.

"Yes. Detective Bobby Macaulay. Who is this?"

"My name is Melissa Grant," she said, just above a whisper.

My instincts immediately took over. Still, I could barely contain myself.

"Melissa. We've been looking for you, honey."

"I don't have much time. I am going to make a run for it."

"Whoa, whoa, do we have time to talk for a minute or two?"

"Just," she said.

"If you leave your cell on, I can get to you. I can have the call traced."

"You don't understand, there isn't time for that. He'll see one of the phones is missing."

"Your dad?"

"Yes. I have to try now. Believe me, Macaulay, I've thought this through."

"Do you know where you're at?"

"I've never been outside," Melissa said. My heart ached for this girl.

"Do this," I said. "Give me ten minutes. Put the phone under the bed or somewhere your dad won't see it. I can get my people to triangulate your position that fast. Then you can disconnect and even put the phone back."

"I need to run. You don't understand. I can't be here any longer. I'm losing my mind."

"Take the phone with you, then," I said. "But *leave it on as long as you possibly can.*"

"I can do that."

"I need to switch to my second line," I said. "I'll still be here, baby, and I *will* get to you."

"He just went downstairs, I have to go now. The phone will stay on——"

And with that she stopped talking. I could hear the muffled sounds of a phone being jostled around. I quickly put Melissa on hold and called my tracer unit.

"There's an incoming call on my cell, right now, still connected. I need to know where the caller is—this is top priority over everything else. This is Melissa Grant on the phone."

I didn't have to say anything more than that. The tech team went to work, reverse pinging cell towers, triangulating positions. Eight minutes later they had her.

"Warehouse district," the tech said. "Slauson and 23rd."

I flipped the lights only. I didn't want Spence Grant to hear a thing. He'd probably already be aware soon anyway, but I was actually not far from the warehouse district—ten to twelve minutes if I could manage to get through traffic. Thursday was a popular dinner night in Denver.

I switched back to Melissa. "Are you there, Melissa?"

Still nothing but the muffled sounds of the phone being jostled. Then I heard it. Melissa screamed. But the jostling sounds continued, which meant she was still on the run.

I hit the sirens. Fuck it. The race was on now—with the sirens traffic was much more maneuverable, some cars getting over to the right, others stopping, but that was exactly how we were trained to drive a high-speed pursuit.

Slaloming, we called it. Not every car could get over to the right in the city. And some idiots with their music turned up loud enough to bust an eardrum wouldn't hear us. We practiced this at least three times a year. Some cars stopped. Some still driving, oblivious. Some over at the right, some pulled over to the left.

I made time and I called Dispatch to send the cavalry.

Spence Grant had been gathering things he needed to bring with them. It was time to leave the house of horrors. What they had built—planned and contrived, he and his inner passenger—had served its purpose. The plan now was to take his daughter to the safe-house. After they—

Spence heard footsteps. He stopped and turned an ear toward the upstairs. It was faint, but his senses had become like a cat's. Someone was walking slowly upstairs. And then he heard it. The most dreaded sound of all. Worse than the appearance of his demon.

The alarm went off as the front door was breached.

Spence took the stairs three at a time. By the time he reached the top his guest was waiting for him.

"What the fuck is going on?" the thing said, gurgling. The transformation took time and energy. Sleep.

"I think my daughter just ran out the front door."

Monster and human ran in stride to recapture their prize.

Melissa knew there would be an alarm. She'd never heard it, of course, but she'd heard her father talk about the security system many times. The problem was that she had absolutely no idea how (or even where) to disarm it. This wasn't a typical home system she could simply guess or steal the code.

As soon as she made it outside into the cool night air, she ran. She ran like she'd never believed possible. The adrenaline had her moving fast, but she'd grown to young womanhood in a warehouse—home-schooled, aware only of how many paces to this spot, how many to that.

Turns out Melissa Grant was a bona fide track star and didn't even know it. She reached the edge of the compound, fortified by chain-link only. They obviously had not wanted to draw too much attention to their little encampment of terror. Razor wire might have done just that, she thought, as she leapt for the grid of the fence.

It was at least ten feet tall—a lot of climbing. And just as she began her quest for freedom, Melissa heard both the police siren in the distance and the pair of pursuers reach the front door.

Spence saw Melissa hit the fence running, jumping at least six feet in the air and landing on the metallic wall like a jungle cat, all four appendages spread, hands grabbing the chain-link. And she began crawling like a fucking spider monkey. It was actually impressive and the part of Spence Grant that was still Spence Grant cheered silently for his daughter.

Go, Melissa, go.

But the part of Spence that was monster caused his stomach to triple over in cramps, a tiny reminder of who he was and what his fate and mission had always been.

Spence ran faster. The beast, who was almost completely human now, ran beside him.

"If she escapes, I will kill you," it said, breathing as normally as if it were sitting in a chair, watching television.

In the distance Spence heard the siren. He actually heard it the moment Bobby Macaulay turned it on. And he sensed the detective's approach deep within. Or the humanoid sensed it and therefore, so did he.

Melissa was already halfway up the fence. There was no way they'd reach her before she scrambled over the top. But the sound of the approaching Macaulay was still three, maybe four minutes away.

The presence within Spence Grant reached out, invisibly yes, but with so much influence and power—it reached invisibly for the girl's mind.

Melissa was smiling. The top was moments from her grasp. But what then? Which way to turn? Which road? Should she stay on the road even? Of course she should stay on the road—Macaulay wouldn't be able to—

No. Take to the trees.

There was a huge hill—practically a mountain— behind the warehouse district, a veritable forest of undergrowth and scrub and evergreen trees. Maybe that was a better idea.

It is.

Maybe if she could hide in the trees she could wait until Macaulay arrived and pick her moment.

You can. The trees are your salvation.

Melissa reached the top of the chain link fence, rolled over the top, and jumped into a thicket where the landing would be softer and not so jarring.

And then she left the road and headed for the foothills.

I knew we were down to the most important few minutes of the entire case. My eyes scanned the roadway. Melissa was an intelligent girl. She knew that the road was salvation; the road is where "Macaulay" and she intersected, her running toward the sound of my siren, me driving as fast as I could and not run her over or drive right past her.

I was almost there. In fact, I was a little surprised to have not seen Melissa yet. I could still hear the muffled, jostling sounds so I was pretty certain she was still on the run. We couldn't be more than yards apart at this point, assuming she stuck to the road.

Melissa stopped running. She was deep into the trees by now and realized that in running to the trees, not only was she hiding herself from her rescuer but she was running in the *opposite* direction of his approach.

She looked down at the road just in time to see the blue flashing lights pass her position, at least a half mile away, still heading toward the warehouse where now, certainly, Macaulay would assume she never made it out and begin hunting for her room by room. No one would be stupid enough to choose a direction *away* from safety.

It was then she felt the large, cold, vise-like hand clamp down on her shoulder. She turned and looked into the eyes of a complete stranger.

"Hello, Melissa," the man standing before her said. "My name is Father Rule."

10

BY THE time I arrived at the warehouse, I knew I'd lost her. I sat outside the closed doors of the warehouse in my car as a light rain began to tumble down upon the roof and windshield. There was no rush now. I knew what we'd find inside. Nothing, not any*one,* at least. Just a haunted house where young girls had been tormented, starved, and hanged.

There would be no people and there certainly would be no Melissa Grant. I had lost that race. The brass ring. That one time when fate shows you an opening. It doesn't happen a lot in our line of work, unfortunately, and when it does, a detective better be alert and ready to leap through.

I played the events through again and again in my mind, dissecting the way I handled the surprise situation.

There was no bigger critic of Bobby Mac than me. Yet I just didn't know how else I could have played it.

Tell her to hide somewhere?

Maybe. With a different set of pursuers. But these things—these supernatural beings—would've found her almost immediately. And it was hard for anyone, much less a young woman, to stay motionless, silent, and above all *hidden* for any length of time with people looking hard for her.

I had been close enough that it made sense for her to come toward me. That and the cell phone really—

I grabbed my phone and speed dialed the Tech department.

"Tech."

"It's Macaulay. I lost her, but what about her cell signal?"

"Still pinging towers. We thought you had her; she's on the move."

Smart girl, Melissa. Fucking genius.

Or maybe an accident. Either way—

"She's not with me. You are now tracking an abduction. How long can you stay with her."

"Until she's out of range of cell service or the battery dies," the technician said.

The battery. Burners were notorious for short battery life. The shorter the battery life the more burners you had to buy. Fucking economics.

"Stay with her," I said and disconnected.

This wasn't over yet. I dialed Lieutenant Shackleford and Manny, who should already be en route, in that order.

The man named Father Rule wasn't dressed like a priest, but he looked normal to Melissa. Even friendly. Maybe if she didn't tell him who she was or what was going on, he would eventually lead her to freedom.

As they walked along together she allowed Rule to get just a half-foot in front of her, out of his peripheral vision. She had to hide the cell phone and keep it active until it died. She'd closed it, disconnecting from Macaulay, but she was pretty sure if she kept it powered, it could still be found.

But where to hide it, she thought, as they walked through the forest, ostensibly to safety. It was disgusting but she could only think of one place where they wouldn't look. Melissa slipped the cell from her front jeans and reached down the back of her pants and slid the folded phone in between her butt cheeks.

If anyone looked there, she was in a lot more trouble than she imagined.

"We need to get you out of this cold," Father Rule said. "It's starting to rain you know."

He was walking them away from the warehouse. That was good.

"What were *you* doing all the way out here in the woods?" Melissa said.

"Didn't your parents teach you it is rude to answer a question with a question?"

"My mother is dead and my father is a—a—"

"A what," Rule said. "A monster?"

Melissa looked up into Rule's eyes. They were so devoid of light as to be like holes in his head. A shark's eyes. Marbles. There was no more life to them than that.

"Who *are* you?" Melissa said.

"Who I am will become the most important thing in the world soon," Rule said. "But for you? Now? I am your salvation."

Spence Grant and the humanoid demon hid in the bushes as Detective Robert Macaulay drove by in his car.

"The warehouse is useless now," the creature said.

"I-I'm sorry. I—"

"Shut up," the creature said and backhanded Spence so hard his glasses flew from his head and he stumbled backwards, hit a tree branch with his Achilles' heel, and dropped straight on his tailbone. It hurt like crazy.

"OW," he said.

"Ow?" The creature said, mocking his tone.

Pretty soon you're going to be about as useful to them as the warehouse, Spence thought but did not say.

"I know who you are," Spence said, still sitting on the ground, spitting out a string of blood from a bit lip. "I know what to call you."

"We must go to the safe-house," the thing said. "Rule has your daughter. I can feel it. Time for the next evolution."

"Did you hear me?" Spence said.

"I heard you."

"I deserve to know what the fuck is going on."

"You don't even deserve to be alive."

"At least I'm not a MacAulay," Spence said.

The humanoid fell on top of him and pinned him to the forest floor, its hairless, nearly formed face not an inch from Spence's own. "Say it then. Say it and I will kill you."

"Jackson Macaulay," Spence managed. He wanted to die. It might as well be then.

Nothing happened. The monster stayed there, motionless, silent, breathing its putrid breath up Spence's nostrils.

"I don't care if you kill me, Jax."

"But you will care *when* I kill you, Spencer. Because *when* I kill you, I **will** hear you beg forgiveness for speaking my name aloud."

"And?"

"And I won't grant it," Jax said.

Shackleford and Manny arrived shortly after the Forensics Team, the Violent Fugitive Unit (VTU, we called them), S.W.A.T., a bus—ambulance—and about twenty marked and unmarked police cruisers. Maybe fifty cops.

"You think we have enough firepower here," I asked, a little embarrassed by the overreaction to my call. For the lieutenant, that is. He was the idiot who called all this in; I just wanted Manny and two other detectives.

"God knows what we'll find in there," Shackelford said.

"God forgive us for what we're going to find in there," I said. "But there aren't going to be any warm bodies."

"Bullshit," my boss said.

"Due respect, L-T," I said. "You're wrong on this. And I have Techs working a ping trace—"

Shackleford turned to me and ground his teeth so hard his cheeks pulled on the skin of his face and made him look old and battle-scarred and he seared me so completely not just with his eyes but rather his very presence of self, and, more importantly, of *rank* that I had already decided to stop arguing, whatever he had to say, if anything.

The last thing I wanted was to get in an ego cage match. I needed to be kept on this case; I needed to keep after Melissa Grant, and I could not afford to have a loose cannon boss pull my ass and put me on cold cases for spite.

"My scene, my call," was all he said with his mouth, but his countenance promised the fire of Hell to any man that stood up to him then. I'd already decided to shut up and just be Bobby Mac. No, that's not right. Mac would've punched Shackleford in the face for being such a gregarious farce as a cop and for being nothing but a man in a suit and tie and a desk jockey and then would've gone after Melissa Grant.

As a detective and a professional I played the game by the rules this time. Better to have Shackleford on my side when I really wanted something—when I had a better idea where they'd taken Melissa.

"You're right," I said. "Let's take these fuckers down."

Shackleford actually smiled. So did I and I actually felt a twinge of "better" for the first time in a month.

If you can't be John Wayne once in a while, where's the fun?

The VTU used "Betty Boop" their cylindrical, iron battering ram, with a picture of the cartoon on one side and "May We Come In?" painted on the other. Shackleford ordered only members of our squad, VTU, and S.W.A.T. to enter the warehouse, two by two.

We cleared each room on the main level, one by one, painstakingly at times. The television was left on and almost every light in the place was turned off, except for one small female's bedroom.

We found Spence's room, too, a kitchen, bathroom—clearly the living quarters. Shackleford called in Forensics and gave them the first floor to quarantine in crime scene tape and cleared them to go to work.

"Time to hit the warehouse," the boss said.

We lined up and repeated the same action on the door eight feet down.

There were no lights on in the warehouse. In fact the upstairs was nothing but a gargantuan room filled with shelves and what appeared to be machine parts, an office, a small toilet, and a tall door at the rear for deliveries and pickups. The whole building was fabricated and the floor was planked wood atop hard earth.

"There has to be more," I said.

"Back to the house," Shackleford barked.

We re-searched the main living quarters, this time with more of an eye toward exits that were built not to be found.

"HERE," Manny said, his sidearm and flashlight pointed at a room next to the toilet.

A broom closet with no cleaning products but rather piles of towels that were easily lifted and replaced. Manny had removed a section of the pile and revealed a door. We eased it open, the boss likely much less sure now that we were going to run into anything with a pulse.

A long set of wooden stairs led down to a labyrinth of rooms, anterooms, and, as I feared, an execution chamber. A few of the rooms had clearly been used for housing victims. Each of those had a cot, two dog bowls for food and water, a small portable toilet, and a hangman's noose, perfectly tied, swaying slowly in the vented building air.

Whoever had lived or operated in that place—Spence, his friends, the victims—there was nothing to suggest anyone had cleaned out a single thing from any part of the dungeon downstairs. It would be a rare glut for the Forensics team.

Margaret Duchamp might just fulfill my suspicions and pop a hard one right there.

Shackleford spent the next forty-five minutes lining out each team, giving a trove of uniforms to the special investigators to use as required. As we exited the place I said, "L-T, Manny and I should get on this abduction thing right away. The Tech guys, they still have a signal, last I spoke with them, an hour ago, they were still tracing the movements."

"Why the hell didn't you say that an hour ago?" Lieutenant Shackleford said.

I chewed on my Scottish temper, telling it to SIT, and I said, "You're right. I figured 'who knows what we find here?' I guess."

"When you knew they had a fix on a cell phone?"

"Sir, all due respect. You ordered me to search this warehouse. I asked to leave."

"Next time you ask, give me a reason."

I had to bite my temper so hard it shrieked inside me.

"Yes, sir."

"That was complete bullshit back there, Bobby," Manny said. "You told him—"

"Manny you gotta know something," I said, as we hurried to our unit. We got inside the car and I looked him in the eye in that way that says "you know enough already, I shouldn't have to explain this to you" and told him, "I'm never quite sure with the lieutenant which side we are dealing with, Manolo."

I sped out of the dirt lot and pressed a button on the cell.

"Tech."

"It's Macaulay. Talk."

"We've gotten enough pings and worked the direction of travel to believe they're headed toward the Roxborough Park area. Depending how deep or which way they go, Detective, we may not have more than that for you."

"Thanks," I said. "Call me if anything changes. We're going that way now, about an hour away."

When the call had broken off Manny looked at me with the eyes of the young cop who doesn't want to believe what he's heard or seen. Denial. The first stage of everything.

"W-what do you mean by that, I mean, what you said about Shackleford?"

"Manny, I didn't tell you those stories in the bar that day to unburden myself. I told you because I need a partner who understands the uncommon angles from which we are sometimes forced to attack this case."

"Yeah, I get that."

"Well I'm telling you that I get the feeling sometimes that our L-T is more of a hindrance than assistance in our investigation. I'm not saying why, I'm just saying it so that you'll have your radar up, that's all."

"You think he's a bad cop? I mean, bad, not poor."

"I don't know, Manolo. Honestly I don't have a whole lot past my gut on this one, okay? That's going to have to be enough for now."

"Okay, boss," Manny said.

"The techs are going to lose that burner soon," I said. "The battery's going to die and that'll be that."

"Yeah."

"Nobody ever said you could be a detective without doing some goddamned actual detecting, right?"

"Nope."

"So start thinking about where we should be looking up in Roxborough Park. I'm thinking safe-house, so let's start with the more remote neighborhoods with acreage. You can use that Rand Guide behind the seat. Make a quick list and let's start prioritizing on the way over, okay?"

Just then my cell rang.

"Macaulay."

"Signal went dead," the tech on the other end said.

"Maybe they're in-between towers."

"No, we were getting a weak ping off tower X-ray two five niner and then it just stopped. You move away from a tower it's more gradual."

"Where's tower X259 and what kind of radius are we talking about?" I said.

"Sending you the GPS coordinates of the tower," the tech said. "There's too many factors, Detective. I usually say in a remote area like that, with the amount of rock outcroppings, trees, and other blockage material, the phone—especially a burner—would have to be pretty close."

"Best guess, man," I said.

"Less than a few square miles."

I disconnected and pointed to the street guide.

"Two to three square miles from—" I checked the coordinates on the GPS. "Here."

My finger touched where the X259 cell tower was positioned.

"We're going to find this place," I said.

Manny kept circling and crossing off subdivisions.

Melissa and Rule kept moving through the woods until they reached two vehicle tire tracks worn into the dry earth at their feet. Rule turned them left, away from the main road—away from the police and Macaulay and all the other good people who might help her.

After walking on the makeshift roadway for a mile, a pair of headlights topped the horizon ahead, coming right at them. It was Melissa's father in the passenger seat and a hooded man driving the station wagon. Rule put Melissa in first and then climbed in the back seat with her, pushing her across the car to the other side.

"Turn around and get us out of here," Rule said derisively. "Spencer, you have fucked this plan sideways. We still had work to do at that warehouse. Now we're going to have to centralize our efforts at the safe-house."

"I'll kill him now," the hooded figure said, turning the car around in the narrow space.

"You keep your mind focused on the plan," Rule said. "We're not finished with Spencer yet."

It took over an hour driving over the dilapidated vehicle path through the woods and the ride was very uncomfortable, particularly with a cell phone crammed in her ass crack. Melissa concentrated on remaining in control of her faculties. Macaulay had confirmed her hopes that the cell phone signal could lead him to her once; she was certain it could do so again.

It had to.

It was the only hope that was left to her. When a child is forced to face their own parent (or parents) abandoning them, it created inside them an inherent lack of positive outlook and a consuming fear of abandonment in general. Melissa tried to remember the confidence in Macaulay's voice—how he sounded so certain that rescuing her was not only his priority but also one hundred percent possible.

It had been so long since Melissa had felt any kind of hope or chance that freedom might really be out there for her somewhere. She'd been so isolated from everything. Other than the home schooling and the hourly check-ins to make sure she was still in her room (as if there were anywhere else for her to be), Melissa's father showed her almost no attention and when he did, she could see the deluded, sociopathic desire in his eyes.

He meant to kill her. Or help someone else to do it.

Melissa knew there had been others—other girls—brought to the warehouse, and she suspected they had not left the place alive.

Fragments of memories had begun to jar loose inside her head, like icicles melting and then, without warning, letting loose their grasp and falling to pierce the tender flesh of Melissa's mind with awful remembrances— scenes of brutality and killing.

The victims still remained faceless, but Melissa feared she knew the identities that belonged to the murders that were formulating as memories in her head, and that is why she stopped thinking about negative things and concentrated on Macaulay.

His voice.

His confidence.

The care in his tone—the way she felt safer just speaking with him.

She chose to think of Good rather than Evil. And if all that bought her was a few more days without the nightmares, then that was better than nothing. Because if the people she was beginning to believe were gone *were* actually dead, she didn't care to go on living anymore.

Not without them.

Something had broken loose inside of Spencer Grant. He didn't just feel like himself, he *was* himself. The internal passenger he'd been carrying was gone. Or disconnected. He had no idea what was going on but as they pulled up to the safe-house it was all he could do to keep from crying out in happiness, sorrow, remorse, fear, confusion, and every other emotion that could have possibly assaulted him at that moment.

The feelings he had for the murders he'd perpetrated in Idaho—his beloved wife and daughter—were beginning to consume him, to the point of nervous breakdown. He knew he did not have much time before he would explode. The mind (and heart, and soul, and conscience) could only take so much guilt. For a "normal" man like him—a man who couldn't even buy a fishing license he used to feel so sorry for the fish—the avalanche of remorse and guilt were being held at bay only by his realization that he had this one opportunity to save his daughter and offer up one good thing before everything went to Hell.

Literally.

Jax stopped the station wagon and as the four of them got out of the car, Spence pointed to the house and said, "Police. They've found the house—there, coming from the west."

Both Rule and Jax ran to take cover on the other side of the house.

Spencer turned to Melissa, placing his hands lightly, lovingly, as he used to, on her shoulders. His eyes were swelling with redness and sorrow but he looked straight into her brown, innocent, terrified eyes.

"I don't know what has happened, sweetie. But it's me. At least for the moment, it's your dad. And there isn't time for anything else but for you to run. Go back out the way we came. Run like the wind. I love you, that's all you ever need to remember."

And with that he kissed her deeply, hugged her with all his might, and pushed her toward the road.

Melissa, a stunned look having blanketed her face, knew, too, that this was the only moment. She turned and ran.

It was night and we drove in silence toward the Roxborough Park area, an absolutely gorgeous canyon-like suburb in far southwest Denver where gargantuan spires of orange rock angled and pointed and towered hundreds of feet in the air, looking as if they had simply sprouted straight out of the earth. Some jutted from the ground in groups of three or four spires, others in ridgebacks that looked like mini mountain ranges.

We couldn't see much of anything then, of course, except the rain-soaked road in our headlights.

Manny had identified just two subdivisions that met what we considered the qualifications Rule would look for in a safe place—acreage, isolation, distance from law enforcement—and I drove down the road toward the westward one, a place with houses on ten-acre lots called Canyon Vista. There really was no plan. I had not called for backup yet—my gut said a smaller search by myself and my partner might bear more fruit and not risk scaring away the—

A quarter mile up the road, coming toward us in the headlights, was a young woman. She was running as if her very existence depended on winning the invisible race in which she was competing. I saw no pursuers, but when she was within a hundred yards, I saw it was Melissa Grant.

And still no pursuers.

Not yet.

I blinked hard and looked at Manny, who was grinning white teeth from one side to the other.

"Madre de Dios," he said.

"Amen."

I pulled up next to her and the poor, terrified girl ran right past us, never slowing for a second. I don't think she even saw us, so entranced she was—so intent on putting distance between her and the bad people.

I got out of the car and called to her, "MELISSA."

She stopped immediately without turning around.

"Macaulay?"

She turned around slowly and then, when she realized we were police, that I was 'Macaulay', and that she was finally, after all these years, safe, she ran into my open arms.

Father Rule and Jax came back to where Spence stood. Spence could not meet their gaze and stared at the ground.

"What. Have. You. Done?" Rule was spitting his words, confounded. It was clearly a feeling he didn't appreciate nor one with which he had any familiarity.

Spence Grant did look up then. He looked up with rage stretching his skin taut and his teeth grinding and his eyes on fire. He did not know how he'd been freed, though he knew it had something to do with Jax because Jax was his puppeteer—a part of him. If Jax hadn't let go, then what else explained him being himself again?

All Spence knew for certain any longer was that his little girl was free, if only for now; that he would never again allow himself to be controlled by these monsters; and, that he had absolutely no chance of surviving the rest of the night.

"I let my baby girl go," Spence said directly to Rule. "Is that something you're incapable of understanding?"

Rule stepped forward and jammed his monstrous fingers and hand into Spence Grant's chest, splintering his breastplate as if made of balsa wood, and in one quick, effortless move, pulled from Spencer a mangled, bloody, dead heart. He did it so quickly that Spence was left standing there for perhaps an entire second, silent, a happy smile turning ever so slightly on his mouth, then his oxygen bereft brain caused him to crumple into a heap of lifeless flesh and bone.

Rule said not one word. He tossed the heart aside into the scrub brush like a piece of unwanted trash.

"Don't test me," he said to Jax.

"We'll get her back."

"Oh, *we'll* do nothing of the sort," Rule said. "You will get her back. You know how much depends upon it. But understand this: if I have to do this all myself, I will."

"I know you will," Jax said, and sprinted off into the night.

11

THE DISTANCE seemed longer with the indelible silence. I don't think any of us knew just what to say yet. Melissa sat in the passenger seat, next to me, and Manny rode lookout in the back. I suppose there wasn't a lot *to* say right then. The action that had unfolded told the tale.

We had her.

That was the thought that raced through my mind as if looped on reel-to-reel.

The issue was that I didn't know whether to feel good or terrified. It wasn't as if we'd saved the day. It wasn't an old Western where you scooped the girl up on to your horse and rode into the sunset. In our world the sunset (and every other direction) held danger.

But *like* an old Western, every posse in Rule's command would be after us. Melissa—a sweet, somehow untainted young woman—was *the prize*. And no one would leave us alone until they had it back.

Manny broke the silence when I went west on I-70 instead of east, which would have taken us back to the precinct. "Where are we going, boss?"

He trusted me. I could hear it in the lack of challenge in his voice and demeanor. He never stopped watching our six.

"We need to come up with a solid plan," I said. "And I don't know about you and Melissa here, but I could use a little breathing room and some time to decompress."

"Amen to that," Manny said.

Melissa smiled ever so slightly.

"Bum Garvey has a place up here in Idaho Springs."

"Idaho?" Melissa said, then all ears, her face happy and anticipatory.

"Sorry, honey," I said. "It's just the name of a town. But my friend has a place there where we can have a few hours to get some rest and to figure out what to do next. I promise you, you'll be safe there. In fact you aren't going away from me ever again, okay?"

"Okay," she said, and leaned against the window, perhaps looking out toward the Idaho in her mind—one with a mother and sister to go home to.

I had no idea how much she even knew. It was clear she'd been completely isolated all this time she'd been in Denver.

Ten years.

I'd seen P.O.W.s that had spent six months in isolation that would never be the same again. There was a deadness to the eyes; an absence of information. I couldn't possibly know how she was treated although from what I'd seen back at the warehouse, there had been at least a semblance of "home". Her room had looked more or less like any teenage girl's room.

"Macaulay?" she said.

"Melissa, I'd be so happy if you'd feel comfortable calling me Bobby. Or Mac. My friends call me those and I plan on being the best friend you ever have. Not just now, okay? Forever friends."

She moved across the seat and threw her arms around me and a torrent of tears burst from somewhere deep in her soul. I kept one hand on the wheel and hugged her with the other. "I'm so sorry for everything that has happened to you, sweetie. I am not letting you face anything like that again."

"Thank you, Macaulay. I mean—Mac—I like that." And she giggled just a bit through the sniffling and tears.

"I like hearing you say it," I told her.

She kissed me on the cheek before sliding back into her seat.

"Mac," she said to no one in particular.

I looked in the rearview and Manny was wiping the water from his own eyes.

We pulled off the interstate at an exit just past the tiny mountain burg of Idaho Springs and then took to a dirt road that climbed into the trees, gaining elevation as we went. After about five miles, the road forked and to the right a sign told us there was no outlet. I went right. We continued to climb until we reached the top of a small mountain and the road dead-ended at a gate and twelve-foot fence that would have made the kooks at the Branch Dividian compound in Waco, Texas, jealous.

"Holy shit," Manny let loose. "Oops. Sorry."

Melissa turned around and smiled brightly. "It's okay, Manny. Shit is hardly a bad word anymore."

"I'm still sorry, little miss. Mac's always telling me to watch my mouth. I'll watch mine and you watch his, okay? He swears like a drunken sailor."

I got out of the car and approached the elaborate control center where there was a speaker, a keypad, and a large lever. The lever, I knew, would disable the electricity that ran through the fence—but only after I entered the code.

Once I punched in the sixteen-digit cipher and turned down the lever, the gate slowly slid to the right. I got back into the car and drove through. Sensors registered our passing, the gate closed, and the lever moved back into place.

"Don't ever touch the fence, not anywhere on the property," I said to them.

"I can see why you decided to come here," Manny said. "Holy smokes."

"Holy shit," said Melissa and we all laughed. It felt good to release the tension.

When we reached the large cabin with a full wrap-around deck, I knew Manny then appreciated the true advantage to what Bum had built up there in the wilderness. There was nothing higher than the deck of the cabin for five miles in any direction and no trees obstructing the view, three hundred and sixty degrees.

"You could defend this position against a platoon. A whole company, even," Manny said, mesmerized.

"Wait until you see the arsenal."

At the door were two keypads. I entered a different sixteen-digit code into the first pad and nothing happened.

"Wrong code?" Manny said.

"See that green light down in the corner," I asked him.

"Yep."

"I just alarmed the interior fenceless perimeter. It parallels the fence out there, halfway between the house and it, all the way around the property."

"What does *that* do," Melissa asked. She had the look of a student in school, soaking it all in and completely in wonder.

"The ground is planted with Xenon gas. A hybrid of levels and kind used in state-of-the-art hospitals. Developed by one of the agencies as—believe it or not—an environmental-friendly, twenty-first century knockout, or, KO gas. Instant, completely debilitating, and not only illegal for personal use, sort of Top Secret. So no stories. Bum has friends in high places, but even still, not cheap."

"Jesus," Manny said. "Is this guy—Bum—is he stable? No offense intended."

"I'd trust the man with my own little girls," I said. "To include you, Melissa."

"My friends used to call me Em."

"When I say 'my little girls'," I said to her, "I have triplet daughters at home that are ten-years-old. I want you to know I now have a fourth, Em."

I entered the second code that dis-alarmed the front door only. After we walked inside and I closed the door, it re-alarmed automatically.

"Normally Bum wouldn't use half this high-tech protection. But it's a bit of a conundrum, him working for the CBI," I said. "He's a firm believer in the Second Amendment and the civilian's right to defend against any militia, even homegrown, if absolutely necessary. Beyond that, I've never known a more patriotic soul."

"What's CBI?" Melissa said.

"Colorado Bureau of Investigations," I told her. "Sort of like a state version of the FBI."

She nodded her head and continued into the house.

"Everything inside is safe," I told them.

"Thought you were going to say the furniture was electrified," Manny said.

"Funny guy."

"I thought so, too, Manny," Melissa said.

I had to admit, the first time I visited, that was pretty much my reaction.

Daylight was long upon him but Jax didn't stop running until he'd crossed interstate C-470, miles through the scrub and arroyos where he'd tattered his jeans and bloodied his legs, and went to a strip mall to find a clothing store. He turned the latch on the front door and flipped the Open sign to Closed. There were three employees—Jax subdued, gagged, and tied them, and put them in a rear storage room.

He then walked throughout the store, picking three nondescript t-shirts, a pair of jeans, a pack of underwear, and some good lightweight all-purpose boots. He went back into the room where he had stored his captives.

"I'm going to remove your gags for the moment. If you make a sound at all, even a question, I'll tear out your throat. Are we on the same page now?"

All three women, two of whom were streaming tears, nodded. Jax removed the gags.

"The way this works is I ask the questions. You answer. If you're good at following directions and telling the truth, all this ends fine. You lose a couple hundred bucks of clothing and get to go home to your loved ones. Starting with you," he said, pointing at the woman on the left, "and in order, tell me what kind of car you have here at the store."

Total silence.

"This isn't Simon Says," Jax told them. "Just answer the question."

"I-I have a 2006 Ford Explorer," said the first captive.

Jax nodded and looked at the lady in the middle. "A 1999 Dodge Intrepid," she said.

The third woman had a 2011 Escalade.

"You are the owner," Jax asked and the woman burst into tears. "I did tell one lie, but it's not worth crying over."

"W-what?"

"I'm going to need cash. Not a lot. Just some pocket money. How much is in the register?"

"Maybe a hundred and a half."

"Is there a safe?"

The woman nodded and pointed to an office in the back of the storage room they were in. Jax untied her and pulled her toward the office. When they reached the safe, the woman knelt and began working the combination lock. Inside was a nice take for anyone whose goal was a robbery. Jax took around a thousand dollars in tens and twenties.

He walked her back to the other two who hadn't moved an inch in his absence. He gently pushed the owner down to the floor again but didn't tie her.

"You, with the Explorer. Where are your keys?"

"In my purse. It's the Coach bag and the keys are on a chain with a skunk on it."

"A skunk?"

"It's the character from Bambi. My daughter got it for me. A birthday present her father let her pick."

"Here's the thing," Jax said, putting a gag back in each of their mouths but still leaving the owner untied. "I could tell you not to report this, but we all know once I'm gone, you're going to anyway. I'm not concerned about the robbery, or the kidnapping, but I can't have every cop in the state looking for your 2006 Explorer."

He calmly leaned over and put his hands on the cheeks of the owner. "I am truly sorry, but you're the oldest."

And he twisted quickly, snapping her neck, killing her instantly.

The other two went into muffled hysterics.

"QUIET," Jax commanded.

Silence.

"When you talk to the police, you tell them everything. In fact, you tell them I took all the money and you two divide what's left in the safe. Here's the important part: say absolutely nothing about the stolen Explorer. You, call your husband and get him to drive you home. I will have a police scanner. The first report of a stolen 2006 Explorer with your license plate, I stop what I'm doing, go to the address on the drivers' licenses I am taking with me, and I slaughter everyone I find. And if you're not there, I'm a patient man. Look at your boss."

Jax grabbed the corpse by the front of the outfit and lifted it; the head rolled around in macabre half-circles, as if on ball bearings.

"Believe me, she felt *nothing*. You, with the skunk-loving daughter? I'll skin her in front of you and your husband before doing the same to you. So, you can end up stinking animal carcasses or, split up what I would guess is eight or ten thousand dollars back there and pin it on me. You look reasonably intelligent. The decision is yours."

He then went to the front of the store and fished the keys from the Coach purse and took the licenses of both ladies. He went outside and found the Explorer parked in a spot further from the store than most.

We sat down in the high-ceiling living room with a huge fireplace, cliché light-colored cabin furniture and talked about our next move.

"Here's the thing," I told them. "We just don't know who we can trust. Rule could have half the police department. Hell, sorry, heck, he could have them all by now."

"We're screwed," Manny said.

"I don't think so. I have a theory. Big surprise, I know. But I have been thinking a lot about this. Not just today or the Judas killings, but way back, ten, twelve years. All the stuff I told you, Manny. Em, you probably know things I don't, but trust me, I will tell you the whole story one day, okay?"

Melissa nodded.

"If Rule and the rest of them were capable of doing what they did to Jax, Amber, Spence—sorry, Em's father— then they'd have done it. Why not embody the whole city? The whole country? Obviously there are rules here to this—excuse me, Em—motherfucking game."

"Fuck, fuck, motherfucker, Goddamn, piss, shit, fuck, fuck, fuck," Melissa said. "I'm not a child. I'm almost nineteen. With all the things we have to worry about, the last thing you need to be doing is wasting a single brain cell on speaking politely around me. Deal?"

Manny and I looked at each other, eyes wide, eyebrows at our hairlines—with two, identical "well, whaddaya know?" kind of expressions.

"Deal," I said.

"Si," Manny said. "*Trato hecho, senorita Em.*"

"Thanks for that, Em," I said. "Well this has been a goddamned game since day one. But now I'm thinking of it in *literal* terms. Both times I've faced down these, these— shit, I can't say it myself. This is all so crazy."

"Bad guys," Manny said. "That's what I think. It helps. Let's just agree—we say 'bad guys', we know what we're talking about."

"Some bad-ass bad guys," I said. "But I like it. Em?"

"Works for me." She looked clearly happy to be included.

"Bad guys it is. Okay, every time I've faced down these bad guys, it's always somewhere remote. The mountains. I mean way the fuck out in the middle of nowhere."

Manny looked confused.

"People," I said. "No people. Nothing approaching a town much less a city."

"So you think they can only amass, attack, whatever, away from people?" Manny said.

"That oversimplifies it. There are a lot of people, whether they believe in a god or not, they do—to some degree—believe that everything is interconnected. Energy, right? From Einstein to shit like *The Secret*. Positive energy, negative energy. But when we're talking about actually affecting tangible events—success, failure, *possession*, *bad guys*—what is the key word? What makes energy positive, for example?"

"Belief," Manny said.

"Exactly. What if these bad guys can only feed on the weak-minded, or those who have a predisposition to believe in the whacky paranormal crap. More importantly, imagine the energy created by a city full of naysayers. You could pick one here, one there, sure, but maybe that's why they can't just march down the city streets, thousands of these bad guys, because no one fucking believes in them— at least not yet."

"So can I ask something?" Melissa said.

"Of course, honey, ask away."

"Why, then, would you lead us *away* from the city?"

I laid back in my chair and smiled wide. "A smart one, here, Manolo. Not just a question but the question of the hour."

"Sorry, Mac," Melissa said, "I don't mean to sound ungrateful or accusing or anything."

"It's a great question, Em," I said. "Honestly, I was trying to think of a place no one knew about but that was fortified like a castle on steroids."

We all laughed.

"In all seriousness, we aren't going to stay here," I said. "I guess that's where I'm going with this theory. I'm done taking on these bad guys on their turf. Let them bring the hot sauce *to us*. We need to plan a defense strategy that has the *bad guys* out of their element and *in ours*."

"But what *is* our territory?" Manny said.

"Funny you should ask that," I said.

Jax Macaulay—or whatever he had become after the mountaintop; after directing Spencer Grant through his killing spree in his own brother's precious city, didn't know either his brother or the city well enough to have a decent plan as to where he should start. Well, he knew where he would start. He didn't know where they'd gone; that was the more accurate statement. Since learning the inherent weakness in humans he always knew where to begin.

In addition to actually purchasing a police scanner, he also found a car that looked in decent shape but had not been driven in a long time and exchanged the license plates. Fortunately the owner had kept the car's registration current. He could see in the women's eyes he left behind that they were unlikely to report the vehicle stolen, at least until an idiot husband demanded the one do it, but that would buy him more than enough time.

It would be nearing nightfall, and he drove to the only address he knew in the city.

Manny didn't like the plan to leave his partner and the girl behind but he had his part to play and he was more than a little proud that his heritage would contribute to Mac's plan to end Rule's intent and dominion over the people of Denver and, further, the world.

He arrived at *Mira's* just as darkness was descending.

"Manny Rodriguez," Mira said as he walked in and approached the bar. The place was teeming with neighborhood regulars, most of whom knew Manny but would not show respect because of the choice he had made. He would never be touched or harmed in any way; he was too close to the Colón family for that ever to happen.

"I need a sit-down with your father, Mira."

"Oh, mijo. You know how difficult that will be, given all we've been through. You are guarded but not trusted, Manolo."

"This is a matter of life and death for the *neighborhood*, Mira. For the whole city. I would not ask if it were not important, your father should realize that."

"Give me a few minutes," she said, and disappeared into the office.

Manny ordered a tequila with a beer back. He needed more courage than flowed in his veins at that moment. More than alcohol could provide him, likely, but the drink would help.

He was halfway through the beer when Mira returned.

"Papa is on his way. He wasn't thrilled."

"And that's putting it nicely I'll wager."

"You'd win that bet, mijo. But he has always loved you. My father is an emotional man. As much as he needs you to be gone from this neighborhood—this community—he misses you dearly. This much he cannot hide from his daughter."

"No one can hide anything from you, Adelmira Colón."

"I have my ways just as you have yours," she said.

Twenty minutes later a man the size and shape of a side of beef walked into the bar. All conversation stopped for a moment and then began again, much softer and more muffled than before. Hernando Colón was a King in the Puerto Rican nation of the Calaveras Street projects. His dominion extended throughout "Little 'Rico" and he was a man who was rightfully feared.

The jefe did not acknowledge Manny as he went through the bar to the rear office even though he passed so closely the nervous cop caught a whiff of his expensive cologne. Once Jefe Colón had settled, Mira came for Manny. All the conversation would be in Puerto Rican Spanish and Manny was as nervous about that fact as anything else.

He ordered a glass of ice water to bring with him.

The sweat already ran freely down the nape of his neck.

"Why did Manny have to go?" Melissa said as Mac prepared her a ham and mustard sandwich. "I like him; he makes me feel safe."

"Oh, I get it. Macaulay's not enough for you. Thanks, Em. Thanks a lot."

"Ha, ha," Melissa said. "You know exactly what I mean."

"I know, honey. I do. Believe me, *I* feel safer with Manny here. Problem is, he's the only one that can get the approval and the backup that we need. And this is still the safest place for us to be. I haven't even told Bum—my friend, who built this place—that we're here."

"Your paranoid friend," she said with that half-joking tone.

"Bum believes the world is going to end," I told her. "His exact words to me in building this place—the first time I saw it, feeling a bit like you do—were these: *I don't know if the end will come while I'm still alive, but it'll be some relative of mine, and when it happens, this will become the most logical place on earth.*"

"He makes a good point," she said.

"He's a good man," I said. "You'd like him a lot."

"I hope I get to meet him."

"I do too, honey. I really, really do."

My stomach did a cartwheel in my belly. There were a lot of things I wished for, and unfortunately there was a helluva long, gnarly road between where we were then and the place where all my wishes came true.

Jax sat outside the Macaulay residence, waiting for all the lights to go out. He needed to catch Amanda sleeping. She was too good; too much of a cop. Even he remembered that. He also knew she wouldn't give up any information on her husband easily. It didn't matter. The thing Jax was now—though at times it still felt human emotions like regret and guilt—was prepared to do whatever was required to get Melissa Grant back to Father Rule and his monstrous cronies.

Manny walked out of the office as nervous as when he went in. His Spanish had sucked, he stumbled again and again trying to decide how much to tell and how much to keep hidden. In the end he told Jefe Colón this: *No matter what, jefe, you trust me. I know this to be true. I am telling you there is a terrible plague that will befall this city and, eventually, every other city in the world—which means every Puerto Rican in the world, too. What I ask is more dangerous than anything any of us ever faced growing up on these streets. YOUR streets. But who better to defend the world, since it's come to that, than the proud nation of Puerto Rico?*

"And?" Mira said as he passed her, placing a hand on her shoulder and leaving a lingering kiss on her rose-colored cheek.

"He agreed to help."

Amanda tossed and turned. Normally she did not struggle with sleep, but with Bobby gone God knew where, she'd been on edge every minute of every day it seemed. She dropped a fork feeding the girls that morning and just about gave herself a heart attack.

Woman dies in front of children; cause: a fork.

She had just fallen deep asleep when something pulled her—no, eased her—out of her extremely unconscious state. When her eyes opened, she knew she was dreaming still. Jax stood beside her bed, looking down on her with loving eyes.

"Jax," she said softly. "We've all missed you so."

"I've never been far," he said. "Watching over you all."

Amanda smiled. A good dream.

"I've wished so many times I could have been with you on that mountain—with Bobby. That somehow we could have helped you."

"I know you have," Jax said, smiling. "But you can help me now."

"How can I help you, Jax? You're gone, sweetie."

Jax sat on the bed and stroked her gossamer hair.

"Where is my brother? I want to visit him, too, but he's not with you, where I thought he would be. I want to tell him how much I miss him."

"I don't know where he is," Amanda said.

"The limitations of the dream and spirit world," Jax said, feigning a goodness he did not feel. "Even in finding our loved ones—those we left behind—we are not all-knowing. Not as people seem to think."

"I would tell you, Jax. Bobby misses you so much and his dreams of you are so awful. They torment him. For you to visit and express your true feelings—if you could forgive him."

"I would tell him there is nothing to forgive, that I know more than anyone he did what he always does—everything possible to him."

"There is a place," Amanda said sleepily, drifting back into unconsciousness again.

"Where?" Jax whispered into her ear.

"Bum Garvey….."

Jax stood and released his hold on her and Amanda fell back into a thick, dreamless sleep, unaware that she had just doomed her husband and his best friend.

12

MELISSA'S FAVORITE book in the world, *Watership Down*, happened to be in Bum's massive collection kept in his den in shelves that covered three of the four walls. She was curled in a chair, reading the book for what she said was the eighth or ninth time. I remembered loving the book back in school when we read it, but had not looked at it since.

"I love rabbits," Melissa said. "I once had three—I named them Fiver, Hazel, and Bigwig."

I looked up from my own reading—some scratch paper upon which I had been doodling some of my thoughts, links, probabilities, and other things that had occurred to me that I did not want to forget or overlook.

My phone buzzed and I answered it. It was Manny. He was on his way back to the compound but said he needed me to remind him where to turn because in the dark everything had taken on a completely different look.

Dark in the wilderness is not like the darkness I have seen anywhere else in the world except upon the ocean. People that have grown up and never been far outside the city tend to scoff at people who admit they are "afraid of the dark", but take one of those people and drop them in the middle of the woods at night and at the very least they'd come back with a new appreciation for the ominous potential of true darkness.

I talked Manny in and then handled the various security safeguards for him as he brought the car back into the compound.

"So?" I said once we sat back down. "Did you meet with the big guy?"

"Yes. I felt like a dunce—a court jester dancing before the king—but yes, I was able to talk with him and convince him that to help us would not only be smart, it would forever cement the importance and valor of the proud Puerto Rican people."

"So tomorrow, we leave here after getting some much-needed rest. I'm taking the risk that we can sleep here safely. It won't be much longer than that, though, before Rule finds this place, too."

"Mac, will you stay with me?" Melissa said.

"As if you needed to ask. I told you, I'm not letting you out of my sight."

"Mira asked about you," Manny said. "Ooh, did those 'Rican eyes dance for her Bobby Mac."

I frowned at him and Melissa asked, somewhat dejectedly, "Who's this Mira?"

"I promise, you'll like her," I said. "And Manny needs to tell Mira that Bobby is *married*. To a cop, no less."

"You're married to a cop?" Melissa said.

"FBI," Manny said before I could answer.

"You'll like her, too," I said.

"I like *you*," she said and went back to reading.

Manny raised his eyebrows at me and I pointed a finger right between them.

Bum Garvey was reading the newspaper in his plush outdoor lounger under the light of the porch, sipping a single malt with a Cuban Montecristo number 4 cigar roasting in the ashtray at arm's length on the table beside him. His Smith and Wesson .357 lay on the table, too, also within arm's reach.

"Now you see, that's what I've always hated about this country," Jax said from the shadows, nearly killing the old CBI agent with a jolt to the ticker.

The pistol was in Garvey's hand almost without him realizing he'd swiped it up when he stood, so keen and worn in were his instincts. "GodDAMN it, you scared the holy fuck out of me. Who the hell is that? Show yourself or I'll open a hole in you so big the coroner won't have to make a single cut."

"That's funny," Jax said, and stepped out into the light of the back yard. "But you're still a damnable hypocrite, old man."

"Good Christ, man. What in fuck's sake are you babbling about and who the hell are you?"

"I'm talking about that cigar. You are perpetrating a felony, sir, and you are a law enforcement professional. And who I am won't mean a thing in a few minutes. In fact, it's better for you if you don't know."

Garvey took off the reading glasses from the bridge of his nose and stepped a bit closer to the intruder. "Sweet Jesus, you look just like Bobby Macaulay's brother, Jackson."

"Most folks—especially good old boys such as yourself—call me Jax."

"That ain't possible," Garvey said, "except—"

"Except my brother has shared his innermost secrets with you, just as you're going to share yours with me."

"You must've missed the part about a hole big enough to play a game of Texas Hold 'Em in."

"I have a special affinity for the overconfident."

"I'm the one standing here with a gun, bud—"

Jax moved so fast it really could not be classified as movement. He had disarmed Garvey, put him to his knees, and locked him in a sleeper hold so quickly the CBI agent didn't have time to be surprised.

Then it was—lights—out.

Bum came to tied to one of his own high-back kitchen chairs. He attempted to move his arms and legs—testing the binding job for loose places or weaknesses. He was one hundred percent immobilized.

"I know how to secure someone," Jax said as he reentered the room and retrieved the fileting knife that was lying on the counter.

"Goddamn if you aren't the twin of Jax Macaulay," Garvey said. "I never had the chance to meet him but Bobby keeps a picture of the two of them on his desk."

"You speak of me both as if I'm not standing in front of you and in the past tense, as if I don't live and breathe."

"Jax Macaulay wouldn't have his brother's best friend and a fellow lawman bound in his own kitchen under threat of stabbing."

"You're not under threat of anything," Jax said. "Not yet. If you tell me what I need to know, we're just two good old boys catching up on lost time and this is just a plain old kitchen knife that ended up in my hand by mistake."

"That so? And if I don't tell you what you want me to?"

"Then the threat is nothing nearly as simple as stabbing."

"Like I said, not something Jax would be doing."

"You said you never even met me."

"I knew Jax through his brother, and the person in front of me is not him."

"Fair enough. If it helps make things easier to digest, think of me as Jax version two. Kind of like software."

"They usually make improvements in new versions of software."

"I can see why my brother likes you so much," Jax said. "I already do, too. Bobby told me one time when we were fishing about this incredible cabin you built in the woods. I mean if he was to be believed and wasn't exaggerating, this place rivaled any compound I know of."

Garvey remained silent, staring straight ahead.

"Tell me where it's located," Jax said. "That's it."

"No way."

"If it's as impenetrable as my brother made it sound, I'd think you'd relish the challenge."

"You're right," Bum said. "You'll find it one way or the other and there's no way you're getting through to my cabin whether Bobby's there or not."

"So tell me where it is and we're done."

"Maybe I want to call your bluff on just how good you are at torturing a man."

"Bobby told me you were brave. In fact, I've known too many men like you. You'd be too hard to break. Or you'd tell me the wrong location. You got your Jack Russell, what, two months after Bobby bought his—I'm talking about the cute little guy outside in the garage with the impressive pen you built for him to keep him warm in winter and cool in the summer—what'd you name him? *Rogue.* Love that name and for you, perfect."

"You son of a bitch," Garvey said.

"Here's how it works, Bum: Rogue and I are taking a little trip together. We're going up to your summer cabin. If we get to the cabin, I'm betting Rogue has his own quarters and everything, and that's where I leave him. Food, water, the whole shebang. You keep refusing to answer me, we start off by seeing if Rogue makes a good three-legged dog. You can count backwards from there. If you tell me the wrong directions, on my way back, on the interstate, going seventy miles an hour—Rogue gets to play fetch."

It was three in the morning when I heard the vehicle crunching up the special gravel Bum had covering the last hundred yards into the cabin. Didn't matter how slow you drove—it was annoying as hell.

I silently thanked my friend for his tenacity and genius.

"Melissa, wake up, honey." I'd been snoozing in the uncomfortable chair next to her bed.

"I heard it, too," she said in the near-darkness. "Who is it?" Obviously good quality sleep was still a few years away for her.

"Someone who we're going to be ready to deal with." Just then Manny came silently through the door, gun drawn.

Garvey had installed under-lighting strategically throughout the house. It provided a low-key, ambient light to make your way around at night and see shapes just fine, but did not emanate at all through the one-way glass windows.

"Orders, boss?"

"Whoever it is, they're still a minute or two away. They stopped when they realized they couldn't stealth us in a vehicle. They can't see in at night through the windows Bum installed. We could turn on the lights and have a party—they are specially polarized, like sunglasses.

"Melissa and I will go to the front of the cabin. You take the rear. There is at least one large window and two turret-sized, shoulder-level windows on every wall. The turrets slide open—flip the latch if you need to. The view of the road and anything or anybody is outstanding. There is nothing but fifty feet of open ground from the tree line to the fence, three hundred and sixty degrees and as soon as the motion-detectors are tripped, it'll be daylight out there. The panel here will show us the area of any motion and bring up the video surveillance for that part of the compound.

"Alternatively we've also got the video surveillance room where every inch of the grounds are covered at all times. I think our best move is to identify our visitors and decide the next course of action once the threat is identified."

"Agreed," said Manny.

Melissa nodded, her face a sheet of blankness.

"Em," I said. "Me and you, baby. I go, you go. Hip to hip, okay?"

She nodded again, this time more confidently.

We took our places and waited impatiently for the show.

After about twenty minutes we could hear the sound of the vehicle crunching the gravel, the driver clearly having given up the clandestine approach. I assumed the twenty minutes equaled the formulation of a new plan. That plan was Bum Garvey's Forerunner pulling fully up to the front gate. All the lights came on, but Bum's windows were heavily tinted. I could not make out the driver but he was not as large as Bum, who went a solid six foot-four.

The driver reached out and pressed the intercom. There was a pause before anyone said anything and then:

"Hello, brother."

For the second time in my life the world dropped away from my feet, leaving me suspended in weightless disbelief.

RECKONING

What will you do
on the day of reckoning,
when disaster comes from afar?
To whom will you run for help?
Where will you leave your riches?

Isaiah 3:10, ***The NIV Bible***

13

THERE ARE times in most people's lives where they must face a truth that for whatever reason does not compute as logical or possible inside their own minds. Trauma that has been buried away in a victim's mind many times presents itself (when it finally does) in this way. For example, rape victims that deny they have actually been assaulted sexually too often put the truly savage moments in a place so far inside themselves even *they* know not where to find it even did they desire to.

When, say, a year later, the memories kick down the door behind which they've been denied as truth—as factual reality—and demand their rightful place amongst all memories, good and bad, the return of the images is not unlike an out-of-body experience where the victim is watching a third person entirely. It can be that difficult to accept, much less comprehend.

Such return of the forgotten begins as unbelievable, unreasonable, a complete shock to the system, and more than anything, a life-altering revelation.

But what people find, eventually, is that it is none of these things.

It is a *reckoning*.

A bill come due.

A loss never accepted fully, but rather dismissed by the nervous system.

But whatever form in which it comes or what time of life it chooses, a reckoning is nothing less than a demand for the balancing of the scales of truth.

For some reason, some period of time, perhaps from a completely different lifetime, the unavoidable has finally come calling. Five, ten, or a hundred years, it really doesn't matter. It has come, it has always *been* coming because the debt has always been owed and when the person on whom the weight of the universe has dropped finally regains clarity, the realization becomes clear.

I owe this.

It is mine to pay or the creditor's to forgive, but the most terrifying realization (and comfort, strangely enough) is that there is *no more running.*

It is time.

"Hard to wrap your head around," Jax spoke into the intercom. "I get that, I honestly do. And I'm sorry—I wish it could be under more intimate circumstances but, well brother, it's not. I'm here for my possession and you're soon going to understand that—all shock and family dismay aside—you do not have a choice in this matter."

I reached over and pressed the green button. "My own surprise notwithstanding, you've gone delusional in your absence if you think you're taking *anyone* away from this cabin."

"Do you remember the last time you told me I was your best friend in the world?"

"Labor Day weekend, on the houseboat you rented at Lake Havasu. A long time ago—a long time before you died."

"Well, setting aside your clearly mistaken assumption that I somehow perished, that's exactly right. But you'll be pleased as a peach pit to know I have your *true* best friend—the one you didn't ignore for years on end—right here in the car with me."

"Jax, don't." It was cliché; it would prove ineffectual; it bordered on silliness, but it was all I could say. Half my brain was terrified for my friend, Bum, but the other half—the ruthless one—was sending "all hands on deck" orders to the once dormant platoons of guilt bunked down inside my heart.

"Inspiring, Bobby. Truly so. But if you don't open the gate and allow us entry, I am going to soak Agent Garvey here in water and use a rubber baton to press him against his own electrified fence. And if you turn off the juice, I'm going to douse the man in gasoline and have a little bonfire outside the gate. He's unconscious, by the way. Drugs and a good old-fashioned police beat-down with a baton will do that to a fella."

Manny was by then at my side. "We can't let him in," he said.

"But we can't watch Bum fry. I have no compunction at all that he'll do it and he'll do it as he dances a Scottish jig."

"Bum would want you to save the girl," Manny said.

Melissa looked at me with that doe-eyed "you swore" look.

"Bum is the reason I'm taking the risk. I think we can still get out of here. And let me make something clear to *you, too*, partner: Em is never going back to the bad guys. *Never.* Not if it means sacrificing you, Manolo. You satisfied?"

"Sorry, boss."

I punched in the code and the gate slowly slid open. Jax drove the Forerunner through the opening and toward my parked squad car. Halfway there, Jax's window still down, he drove through an infrared beam and five holes in the driveway spewed Xenon gas from the ground beneath the truck.

Jax didn't even get the window halfway back up before the Forerunner rolled left, down the sloped embankment, and crashed nearly harmlessly into a boulder.

"We've got about half-an hour. And since I had no idea if the gas would work on whatever Jax has become, I can't even count on that. Em, you gather our things and grab every piece of armory I laid out on the kitchen in bags. Manny you and I will secure Jax ASAP. Then we load him in my car."

We didn't have to wait long to leave the front of the cabin as the Xenon dissipates quickly and naturally into the atmosphere after discharge. Melissa loaded the guns, ammo, and other sundries into the back of the Pathfinder while Manny and I handcuffed and bound Jax's chest, legs, and ankles where he sat, in the driver's seat, and then struggled to move him into the rear of the Crown Vic.

"Melissa and I will drive Jax to the FBI. I'll call Amanda on the way and have her meet us there. I'm going to gamble on trusting her team. They can secure him and Melissa."

"But you said you weren't letting me leave your side," Melissa said.

"Amanda is twice the cop I am," I told her. "I'd trust her with my life. I *am* going to trust her with yours. Where I'm going, I can't take you. I might as well take the fly to the spider, Em. You have to trust me. You'll be safe with Special Agent Macaulay and her team."

I hoped using Amanda's name might help. From the look on Melissa's face, it didn't.

"You trust me, don't you? That I'd never do anything I didn't think was best for your safety?" I said.

Melissa nodded.

"This is what I believe will keep you safe."

"Okay, Mac," she said, a bit more confident than before. It would have to do.

"Manny. You get Bum to a hospital and then meet me at the parking garage we identified. You're sure your friends will be there?"

"They're not my friends," he said, "but they'll be there. Best back up in the city next to our brothers in blue."

"Bum's not going to be happy, staying behind. He's going to wake up wanting to do things by the book."

"I'll tell them he needs a twenty-four hour psych eval," Manny said.

"Nice. Time to jet."

Manny nodded and jumped in the Forerunner. Melissa and I walked over to my unmarked, Jax still unconscious in the rear, doors locked, fortified steel between him and us.

"It scares me, riding with him," Melissa said.

"Think of it this way: cops in the front seat, bad guys in the back."

"Can I get a badge?"

I handed her mine. "You keep it safe for me, okay? Now it's me trusting you."

That got me a smile.

14

MEYER HAD slept through Jax's visit to the Macaulay residence and the sleeping interrogation upstairs in the master bedroom. He'd arrived the day before and Amanda had picked him up at Denver International. She hadn't been happy to see him but he forgave her. His presence never meant good things, he understood that. He *was* hoping someday that might change.

It was close to noon and he was just getting dressed after finishing the first truly hot shower he'd had in three months. There was a soft knock at the door.

"You decent in there?" Amanda said.

"One second," Meyer said, and put on a polo shirt that was quickly tucked into his jeans. No official business today. "Sure, come in."

Amanda opened the door and handed him a steaming cup of coffee with cream. "I just heard from Bobby finally."

"Thank God," Meyer said. "Where is he?"

"He's on his way to my office."

"The FBI?"

"Yep. Said he needs my help and he wants you to come, too."

Meyer was jetlagged beyond reason and would much rather have crawled right back into the comfy downstairs guest room that doubled as his cousin's home office. He swigged the hot coffee. "I'm ready when you are."

"There are scones on the table downstairs. I just need to grab my cell, badge, etcetera, and then we'll take off."

Meyer turned to leave and Amanda followed. On her way out she noticed Meyer's used towel lying in a crumpled mess on the wood floor. When she leaned over to pick it up, she glanced at the tattered sticker on his luggage.

Missoula International Airport.

Melissa was quiet driving back to the city, probably wondering the same thing I was: when would my brother wake up? We were a few miles from the city limits on top of Lookout Mountain cruising fast with lights on down Interstate 70 when our curiosity was ended.

"Brother. You never told me about the countermeasures. Smart man," Jax said, still sounding groggy from the KO gas.

"Can't take credit," I said. "Bum made the upgrade after our fishing trip."

"And it wasn't like we were Facebook friends or anything deep like that."

"Who the hell are you?"

"I'm your brother," he said, laughing. "Who else would I be?"

"You don't sound like Jax. You look like him, but not quite. What are you, some kind of duplicate?"

"People aren't their bodies or their voices," he said. "Listen to you, always the thinker. You should have read more of the Romantics. Less Asimov and Nietzsche."

"If you were my brother, I wouldn't have to cuff and hogtie you like a common dirtbag."

"You need to because you're finally coming around, not because I'm a criminal."

"Coming around?"

"Stop talking to him," Melissa whispered. "I don't like him. He sounds like my dad did."

"Daddy's dead," Jax said.

Melissa spun around in shock and anger. "Fuck you, you—*dirtbag*."

"Nice mouth," he said. "Maybe Rule was right to tear old Dad's heart out and show it to him."

I hit the brakes, skidding to a stop along the shoulder of the Interstate. I turned around and drilled my own eyes into his.

"You say another word to her and I will come back there and KO you myself. Talk to me or no one at all."

"So I can tell *you* how her father went out like a sniveling coward?"

I got out of the car, opened the back door, clutched the fabric of his shirt, and began pummeling him with my fists. Over, and over again until he was bloodied and broken and barely conscious. "Say it again. Come on, do it. I'll fucking kill you and leave you in the trees for the scavengers, you demon cocksucker."

Jax lay on the backseat, silent but for the spitting of blood from his tattered mouth. I waited. I wasn't kidding.

Nothing.

I got back in the car and drove back onto the roadway.

Melissa looked horrified and I knew at that particular moment there wasn't anything I could do to wipe away the terror because she was likely as scared of me as of anyone else.

We reached the office of the Denver FBI just after Amanda. She didn't need to explain the Melissa Grant situation, even to a team of accountants with weapons. I shouldn't have been so hard on them or glib, but I couldn't shake the inexplicable surety that whatever happened in the next twenty-four hours was either the end or the beginning of everything. I needed law enforcement I could trust and I needed them in force.

That was the next stop. I could not risk climbing any further up the FBI chain; I had already asked too much of Amanda, essentially harboring a kidnap victim (although I had not told her what I knew—or at least suspected on good authority—about Spencer Grant, most-wanted).

"Meyer," I said, and embraced my priest cousin. "I've missed you."

"And I you, Bobby."

"I need you to come with us," I told him.

"Bobby, only you can wield the weapon of our ancestry."

"You know that's not true. You can't have forgotten Tilson Wayne. Any member of our clan—"

"You and I both know that a cousin is weak blood at best, and that I am too much of a weakling and, I admitted, a coward, to do what must be done."

"Meyer, that's just not true."

"It should be you, Bobby. Under the circumstances," he slid his gaze up and back, toward Jax, or whatever he was.

"Then you, old friend, are charged with keeping my girl here safe." I pulled Melissa to me. "You'll find no more trustworthy a man, even if he is a priest," I told her.

"Count on me for that. I've got the best cop in the city with me," he said, smiling at Amanda.

I turned to her. "We can still rearrange this. We haven't gone too far, not yet."

"Don't even think of pulling me out of this," she said. In addition to loving me, she'd watched her comrades die mercilessly at the hands of our bad guys.

"Just thinking of you and your career," I said.

"I know."

I kissed her and grabbed Jax by the cuffs and led him out into the descending night.

"You want *what?*" said Len Brighton, sitting behind the desk at the S.W.A.T. and Violent Fugitive Unit headquarters.

"You and a dozen men and women you'd trust with your family's lives."

"Bobby. You know I respect you, but—"

"Len, you've now seen some of what I have. I know you trust me, though you might have a hard time admitting it. These creeps hurt Bum Garvey. They've killed children. But I need this off the clock."

Len was old–school. He was too much like me and I was counting on that cop factor, way down in his soul. The law enforcement officers, or LEOs, who cared about justice above protocol.

"I have a dozen, maybe a few more," he said. "But my guys are worth three of yours any day of the week."

"I don't doubt it for a second," I said.

I gave him the coordinates of the abandoned parking garage. "I just need an external perimeter. Containment. But it may not be easy."

"Walk in the park," he said, but I heard the tremolo of unease in his voice.

I had one more call to make.

As I drove Jax, my brother, the *thing*—I didn't know what to call him—across the city, he was silent for a while and I was grateful. Too bad it didn't last.

"I'm not myself," he said, and I took it as a poor attempt at humor.

"Fuck you."

"Nah, not this time, brother. I mean it. It's me and you. I'm sorry for all this. I don't understand it much more than you."

"I doubt that. Tell it to the dead women."

"Spencer Grant killed all those women, and he would have killed his own daughter if—"

"If?"

"Never mind. I never was any good at convincing you, was I?"

"We're light years beyond those days, Jax."

"We're never beyond those days, Bobby."

15

"I'M SORRY about all this," Amanda said from her desk, Melissa sitting in an extra chair in her cubicle.

"You're Mac's wife?"

"Yes."

"And an FBI agent?"

"Yep, that, too."

"I want to be an FBI agent."

"I think that would be really cool," Amanda said.

"Cool?"

"It's an admirable endeavor," Amanda said. "I'm sure you'd make an excellent one."

"Mac saved my life."

"He's good at that."

"Has he ever saved your life?"

"He saved me when he married me," Amanda said, uncomfortable with the young woman's fixation on Mac. Hostage and kidnap victims often developed feelings for their rescuers. The level and volatility of said feelings ranged vastly, depending on circumstances. Amanda couldn't imagine many circumstances worse than what Melissa had endured.

"He loves you," Melissa said flatly.

"He loves you, too, Melissa. He wouldn't have left you with anyone else but me. That should tell you something."

"What, that you're this amazing policewoman and can protect me as well as him?"

"No. Because he trusts me with his life, so he trusts me with yours."

Silence.

Meyer poked his head around the doorjamb. "Everything copacetic in here?"

"We're good," Amanda said. "There's coffee so bad it's a police cliché in the break room."

"Already sampled," Meyer said. He winked at Amanda. Situation diffused for the moment.

"So, Cambodia?" Amanda said to Meyer.

"What? Oh, yes. It was heartbreaking. So many lost."

"Did you go with the church or the Red Cross."

"Uh, both, actually."

"Long flight?"

"Ghastly. And the Vatican knows not of Business Class."

"Is that a straight flight to DIA or do you have to change planes on the coast?"

"LAX. Los Angeles. Thank the heavens *that* is a short hop to Denver. Comparatively speaking, of course."

"Yeah, that's not a bad trip," Amanda said, poking around on her computer.

"Well, you ladies stay comfortable and safe. I must attend to my bladder. Coffee, as they say, is rented only." Meyer scooted away and Amanda did something that made her sick inside:

She ran a background check on Father Meyer West.

I convinced Jax to give me Rule's number. He knew my plan, or the idea behind it anyway. If we lost—and by "we" I didn't just mean myself, Manny, and his group, but Amanda, Melissa, Meyer—everything good we'd ever known—a phone call to Rule wouldn't matter one way or the other.

It was time to cross that line that could never be re-crossed. Not with things being the same, anyway.

"MacAulay," Rule spat as he answered the phone.

"I have your puppet," I said. "But I have the girl, too. Time to end it."

Silence on the other end of the line. I continued.

"I'm sending you an address. It's an abandoned parking garage in a run-down part of the city. I want to meet you there. You make my brother whole again—you give him back to me—and I'll turn over Melissa Grant."

"Bullshit."

"If I see even one of your stooges, I turn around and Melissa goes into protective custody and Jax will never see the outside of state prison. I don't know why you want her, clearly her father wants her, whatever you two have cooked up I no longer want my family to be a part of it. I don't care if that betrays some worn-out history. I have a wife and three little girls. Even you can understand that. Give me back my brother and swear to me that you'll leave the MacAulay name alone for good. No more or less than what you plan for anyone or anyplace else."

More silence. This was not an offer he'd considered.

A betrayal.

"Send me the address."

"Swear it to me."

"I swear. I can give you your brother back to you, just as before. You swear you'll give me the young woman and then stay out of my, business, shall we call it?"

"I swear." A lie to a liar is no lie at all. "You meet us there in an hour."

"If I see any police, you know I can add more bodies to the agenda," Rule said.

"One hour and I will send you the address."

"Send it now."

"Trust is a fragile thing," I said. "Let's not create opportunity for a break so soon."

"If you don't trust me, this whole happenstance is a farce."

"No, I just want time to get to the location. That's it."

"Fair enough. You're up to something, but I'll see to your conditions. Many a hand of poker has been lost by the surest of players."

"One hour."

I called Manny. "Are you in place?"

"Si, jefe."

"Tell your people I have a small presence of personal police. Off the clock and of no threat whatsoever to them. Just the opposite, in fact. We'll likely all be happy they're with us."

"No problem. The team here will understand. It won't be the first time they've dealt with the *policía* on friendly terms."

"Notwithstanding, everyone sticks to the plan."

"Agreed, boss."

Melissa had asked Amanda what she was doing and when she realized the agent was engrossed in her work, she decided to take a walk around the place. Not very impressive for the FBI, she thought. They always made things look more elaborate in the movies and on television, two of her very few outlets to the outside world as she grew up, though her father had taken his home education responsibilities seriously.

She had no idea why. He only intended on killing her, just like all those other young women. She'd known that for years and had actually come to accept it in a life's destiny kind of way—just the way things were. Part of it was the constant fear. It became so natural to be afraid that she never really thought about leaving.

Only with budding maturity had her plan to escape evolved.

Melissa also did not know how to feel about her father's alleged death. Part of her wanted to believe what the man named Jax had said. Part of her—the little girl inside—wanted her dad. She wanted him back whole, like the man she had fleeting memories of in her head.

She still could not move further down that path of memories, however. She knew what had happened to her mother and sister and she knew her father was the guilty party, just as he was guilty of murdering all those innocent women in Denver. It was different then, though; she then understood more of the truth; a truth that *sounded* more like a movie plot than reality.

If she clung to that bizarre possibility, however, it meant her father—her *real* father—had not committed those heinous acts. It meant something else had occupied his body. Melissa wondered if it was what they meant by an insanity defense.

"Surprise," Father Meyer said as she walked around the corner into a darkened hallway in the trance of deep thought. She startled and jerked away, as if to flee.

"I'm sorry," Meyer said, placing his hand on her shoulder to calm her.

"It's okay," Melissa said, more relaxed. "Amanda is too busy on her computer to talk."

"Yes," said Meyer. "That's why I'm sorry."

"What?"

"Well, she's going to dig, and dig, and then dig some more. That's what they do, the FBI. And she's going to find out I was never in Cambodia."

"You weren't ever there?"

"She already knows I didn't fly in from LAX. It was stupid of me, really."

"What was stupid?"

"Leaving the tag on my suitcase. I'm afraid I'm not a very good criminal."

"You're not a criminal," Melissa said, starting to tremble despite her confidence that this man was her friend. Mac's friend. "You're a priest."

"She's going to find that out, too. That I'm not a priest, I mean."

"Are you even Mac's cousin?"

"Oh, *that* I am," he said, closing the space between them in an instant and clubbing her at the back of her skull.

Then nothing.

Amanda was oblivious to everything but what she was finding on the FBI computer. No record of a Meyer West at all. She had placed a call to the local catholic church office and asked for a report on Father Meyer West. Ten minutes later the priest with whom she'd spoken called back and said there was no Father West. Not just *Meyer* West; there was no West in the papal directory.

She knew he could not have flown without an ID to match his identity so she contacted the airline for the manifests for all flights the day before between Missoula, Montana, and Denver.

No Meyer West.

Shaw Macaulay.

Amanda ran a check on Shaw and found very little.

No criminal record but for an arrest warrant and subsequent dismissal of charges stemming from the case of an abducted neighbor.

In Priest River, Idaho.

That fucking son of a bitch, she thought. He played his role to perfection. Foil. Intelligentsia. Always there to feed Mac a pellet when he pushed the lever. It would break her husband's heart to learn that the friend he thought replaced his brother was—

Amanda looked up from her oblivion to see Melissa had left the cubicle.

"Melissa?" she called out.

No answer.

Amanda drew her sidearm and with it, double-gripped and angled toward the floor, moved around the right side of the cubicle exit, clearing the six-foot high cube hallway in both directions. It was then she noticed the absolute silence. Not even an office murmur.

She moved from cubicle to cubical.

Each occupied cubicle contained a fallen comrade. Amanda stopped checking cause of death after the first two; each kill was the same M.O.: a knife insertion just below the center skull, severing the brainstem. Silent. Painless.

Amanda fought to contain her emotions and be a cop.

It had become late enough that her team was the only remaining on that floor—that area being comprised of operational units of lesser time-sensitive investigations that rarely worked twenty-four hour shifts.

There was no life remaining where she was and both Melissa and Meyer, or, Shaw Macaulay, were gone.

She'd failed.

Her team.

Young, terrified Melissa.

Bobby.

She pulled her cell from her pants and punched the speed dial to "Mac". It went straight to voicemail.

Shit.

She left a message detailing what she'd found. Concisely. Professionally. Then she grabbed her keys and ran for the elevator.

We arrived at the garage just after I sent the address to Rule—the building was in decent shape, nondescript enough, no presence of anything or anyone as we entered the ground level. We slowly circled, floor by floor. I spotted two of Brighton's finest in the shadows on the fourth floor, halfway to the top, but only because I knew that was where he'd instructed them to stake out. The other dozen or so, plus Brighton himself, would be outside, undetectable, on the perimeter of the garage, with instructions to let no bad guy make it in or out of the garage alive.

There were a hundred Puerto Ricans backing them up, dug into the shadows and niches along the surrounding streets only they knew. Probably armed better than S.W.A.T. That was simply the reality in which law enforcement lived. The hard streets were little different than third world capitals where angst and inequities and arsenals ruled the land.

This was one of the few times that fact made me feel a little better.

When we reached the top floor, Jax still in the rear and silent, the night sky opened to us, myriad points of light, perhaps showing us the heavens, maybe just balls of long-distinguished heated gases.

From the shadows of the flat, open space—all along the perimeter—we would be able to see in all directions. I stopped in the middle of the plateau, twenty feet from where Father Rule stood, alone, as promised (though I knew from experience he was never truly alone).

"You indicated just the two of us," he said without conviction, almost as if bored already of the entire affair. "Promised or swore, if I remember correctly."

"We both knew neither of us would come alone. That doesn't change the stakes at all. In fact, I'm pretty sure this drama is playing out exactly as it's meant to."

"But I see no Melissa. That changes things very much. I'm sure, however, you brought along that pathetic toy."

"That 'toy' has been your undoing more than once," I said, something I could never have believed without seeing it firsthand—without using it myself. The Crucifix of Ardincaple lay on the seat, unwrapped from its cloth; a sword and talisman, just a reach away.

I opened the back door, untied and un-cuffed Jax, and pushed him toward Rule. He stumbled a bit, walked a few steps, then stopped halfway between us. "I don't want him back," I said. "I don't take betrayal lightly and neither should you."

"Yes, the mercy he showed young Melissa. Very disturbing. I suppose no one can trust a traitor, even the other side. It's a wonder your wife trusts you."

"You're not going to get to me this time, Rule. Whether you want to accept it or not, this is where it all ends."

"Or where it all begins," he said, sneering.

Manny rose from the shadows and joined me.

From below I could then hear the subtle squealing of rubber tires rounding the parking garage pavement inside, climbing toward us, already, it seemed, past all lines of defense, including the fourth floor S.W.A.T. members.

Why had no one challenged the driver?

As if in answer to my thoughts, an unmarked police car with tinted windows drove slowly out to park ten feet behind me. Meyer got out of the vehicle and scampered over to where I stood.

"Coward or no, I stand with you, cousin," he said.

"I'm glad you're here," I said.

Manny nodded.

I thought I heard a muffled cry from behind but before I could react there began a crescendo of automatic weapons fire from below, further out than Len Brighton's S.W.A.T. perimeter. I removed my sidearm and sidestepped over to the wall, which was really two walls, the most interior meant to safeguard against a rogue vehicle breaking through the outer.

Below, at first just in the distance, but soon from everywhere, out of the darkness and shadow, came the demons. They were black as coal, misshapen, and under the cover of night, in a poorly-lit area of the city, nearly invisible.

Out on the surrounding streets, the outer perimeter, the gunfire from Manny's neighborhood men and women raged. Manny joined me against the innermost wall and in my partner's terrified stare I could see that he now believed fully—no one could, honestly—they could not give their minds over to the awful truth until facing it themselves.

The battle had certainly begun. I turned and looked at the demon Rule and he remained a fixture of confidence, smiling, knowing what I, too, knew: that it was a matter of time. A few minutes after the gunfire on the external a block away started, S.W.A.T had opened up on both those demons that broke through the initial lines and more that were then coming from the blackness all around them.

I heard Rule laugh behind me.

Not yet, I told myself.

I looked back at Meyer. He had removed the Crucifix of Ardincaple from the car seat and was holding it in both hands. The blade, the hilt—nothing. Just a piece of metal. Maybe he was right; perhaps only some from our lineage could—

My attention was drawn back to the battle.

The sheer magnitude of heavy caliber munitions (and a cache of explosives rigged strategically throughout the area) had at first begun to overcome the hundreds of monsters, their living, breathing shells being shredded and left useless, littering the ground below.

But Rule cried out, summoning more, and the sky above thundered down its answer to him. More and more demons of all sizes and shapes kept pouring forth and as they pushed forward, getting within reach of the brave humans, the weapons lost their power and none were a match for the physical prowess of the evil creatures.

The diminuendo of gunfire juxtaposed against the rising cries of human terror and agony, were telltale. We were losing and losing fast. I looked at Manny and nodded.

"PARA PATRIOTISOM DE PUERTO RICO," Manny shouted above the chaos.

And from the space between the walls three hundred heavily-armed 'Rican comrades stood as one unit, lining all four sides of the rooftop, and began firing short, controlled, damaging bursts from their automatic rifles.

They knew they had the elevated ground. They knew the importance of Manny's words—that we'd come here for a final stand—and they fought like warriors from a distant time.

Focused.

Undeterred.

Brave and fierce, they cut down the enemy beneath them.

It made a difference. As I'd hoped, the tide turned. Brighton and his S.W.A.T. team retreated to the garage, and, along with the two on the fourth floor, joined the army above.

It was something to see. Gang members and S.W.A.T., side-by-side, fighting for not just a country or a color or a flag but for us all.

Then, like a blue and red lightning storm, Bum Garvey and fifty vehicles from I don't know how many LEO agencies arrived on scene, approaching from all directions, and immediately began a flank assault on the demon army. Vehicle doors flew open and veteran Colorado LEOs opened fire from behind.

Knowing their own comrades were above, they waved the remaining neighborhood platoon back to join them and then launched grenades and tear gas canisters into the horde. Slowly they pushed the demons toward the gunfire that rained down from on high, tightening the noose.

Some of the monstrous beings reached the stronghold, however, and were scaling the cement walls of the garage as if made of pliable earth, their claws sinking into the concrete as easily as with grappling hooks or ice axes.

Manny's people picked them off, one by one, with impressive accuracy, repelling any that gained the walls. It could have been a castle of old; all we needed were archers and huge pots of boiling tar.

Manny and I ran back to join Meyer as Rule bellowed again, calling for more with even his last breaths.

Manny, Meyer, and I faced him—he looked as if he could still annihilate the world with his confidence. Jax still stood between us, as if unsure what to do.

"I could summon forth a million," Rule cried above the mayhem. "Ten million."

"No more," I said, tears streaming down my face. "Not anymore you can't."

I reached toward my cousin and he handed me the Crucifix of Ardincaple—my ancestor's weapon, talisman of the Clan MacAulay for perhaps as many as a thousand years. In my hand, it warmed to the touch. As I raised it toward the sky, it glowed increasingly until it illuminated the entire rooftop.

The gunfire had died down, the demons beaten, and Rule stood statuesque and silent as he waited for the inevitable. The moment had arrived.

The beginning or end of everything.

I then noticed the stars could no longer be seen; a cloud as I'd never witnessed had at some point formed above us, as dark purple as a fresh bruise, with blackened boils and taut swells that looked infected, filled with plagues and threatening to burst. The exterior of the monstrous thing billowed into a macabre musculature that engulfed the sky.

The wind picked up, first swirling randomly, then rotating in a clockwise, circular motion. It gained velocity and strength. The light from the talisman seemed to dissipate, as if in anticipation of the titular moment.

A moment I'd been dreading for too long.

A moment that seared my insides as if lava flowed in my veins.

A moment that was not in question but a necessity of the ages.

The betrayer had to die.

Jax turned toward me. My brother. Or the thing that pretended to be him. Whatever he'd become; whatever Rule and all the Evil in the Universe had conspired to make him, stood not eight feet away.

He stared at me much the way he'd done before in our lives and at that instant—in *that* moment—he looked like my brother. The brother who I'd once loved more than life, than myself, than my father or even my mother.

The brother who, at eight, had been defiled by a *nineteen-year-old* cousin, while I, my brother's keeper, his older sibling—his protector—hid in the shadows, trembling with a cowardice from which I would spend the rest of my life running.

The brother who saw me hiding in the darkness and never said a word for fear of me being hurt but who never took his stare from my eyes, even as he screamed for help.

This much I had remembered as we talked, driving to the parking garage. But I had not known what it really meant, not until Meyer picked up the talisman of our ancestors; not until I saw that the sword had no use for him.

I turned and drove the blade of the Clan MacAulay deep into Shaw Macaulay's chest. He howled and I stared into his eyes as I pushed it deeper.

"I know who you *are*," I said to him, tears still running down my cheeks. "How? Why, you evil fucking bastard?"

Shaw Macaulay didn't answer me. He couldn't, not with the blood filling his lungs and the fire of Ardincaple searing through his tendons and bone and flesh.

The furor of wind had grown even louder and had then begun to form an inverted twister, whose force increased exponentially, and yet none of us moved, nor any object—not so much as a dried stick or a piece of dust—was disturbed.

Meyer—Shaw—fell to his knees as the fire consumed him from the inside. He died without a word of remorse or regret but only a frozen look of shock as his own reckoning arrived. And when he (or whatever he was) did die, his evil soul—ephemeral and at the same time translucent and obsidian as the darkest black hole—was sucked clean of his human shell and pulled skyward into the cloud from Hell.

Then the rest followed. All the demons—dead most, but some still clinging to what they thought of as life—were consumed by the whirlwind and whisked away to the imprisonment that awaited them. All this without anything of this world moving an inch.

I looked at Jax just as Rule reached for him but the demon's hand could not touch him—some un-seeable force kept the demon master away—and a black soul rose, too, from my brother, leaving behind just Jax. He did not die as I had feared but rather dropped down to a knee and covered his face with a thick, callused hand.

Lastly, the cloud, pregnant with malice and evil and all manner of pestilence, finished the taking back of its own.

One more soul to claim.

One last piece of shit to knock the fuck out.

Rule cried out like the ultimate coward he was, but could not be heard as he was drawn like a rocket skyward, spiraling into the maw of eternal nothingness.

Epilogue

I'M NOT sure why I remembered the terrible event that occurred that chill October night when I did. It happened in our backyard, by the garage, but my mind and my guilt buried it so far beneath everything else that it would not playback until years later, I suppose, just when it needed to.

Of course, its very existence inside—the horrible guilt and rage and shame—it fueled me; it was the unknown drive behind likely all I'd accomplished or become since that night. It was the crude oil fuel that raged inside the furnace of my soul and never let me forget my coordinates, my path through my life.

When Shaw Macaulay returned into my life as Meyer West, he looked nothing of the drunken, sadistic, pederast piece of shit that entered our lives back then as quickly as he left. I simply had no memory of him, though had he not changed so much physically, perhaps—

I don't like the excusatory parlance of Coulda Woulda Shoulda. What we've done before—the past—it is not unlike a rearview mirror in comparison to a windshield. We must only check it from time-to-time to verify our bearings, but what lies ahead of us, what spreads out before us in the future, is all we can control.

As I drove Jax to the parking garage that night, I told him I'd remembered, and that it should have been *me* that the monster, Rule, inhabited, and who God forsook. We talked again, like brothers, and he told me there was always something inside him that promised there was a reason and that's why he stayed quiet all those years, never even asking Paddy about our cousin.

He also told me he'd never forgiven me because there was nothing to forgive. He said all he could think the whole time was that, were it Bobby in his place, Bobby would never want him to expose his hiding place and subject a second child to the cretin Shaw. He said that after all the years of me standing up for my little brother, he made himself into a hero for finally protecting me.

I told him he didn't "make" himself into anything, that he *was* a hero, but that I should have tried to stop it nonetheless.

Amanda arrived too late, thank God, and my phone I never did find again. Manny's people—those who survived—buried their own and I heard from my partner that church attendance was up so high that new buildings were breaking ground soon.

I don't know what the other officers and agents thought. We sure as hell didn't talk about it. Over the months, even the whispers disappeared altogether.

Spencer Grant's body was discovered and enough DNA evidence, possessions of the victims, computer files, and a daily diary of his actions, feedings, and kills, to close the Judas case. But there was still the matter of the murdered woman in the clothing store in Littleton. The two remaining witnesses refused to cooperate, afraid of the killer's threats against their families. They were shown pictures of Grant and they said that was not the murderer.

I don't know for certain who killed that poor woman. When I say that, of course I am saying it as the random detective who has not been assigned to the case and has, at best, circumstantial knowledge of particular facts. The department has decided that without the eyewitness testimony, no useable DNA processed from the crime scene, and in my opinion a general distaste for attempting any legal proceedings tied to alleged facts and circumstances outside the realm of normalcy where a jury would be very likely to find reasonable doubt, has decided to place the case in the cold file status.

Jax has a very devoid memory of anything after our trip into the Idaho wilderness. I don't know if or when it will ever return to him. I pray it never does. I've had to explain to him that his wife moved on two years prior and remarried, having grieved for eight years. His daughters are in college, having accepted the death of their father a long time ago. For now the plan is for Jax to stay with us until he figures out what he wants to do. I know some less-than-thoroughly-honest people who nonetheless make the best fake identification I've ever seen.

Another strange leftover from his adventure is that Jax has new fingerprints. I can't explain it, nor do I want to. Given half the chance I would wake up from the past ten years and but for the triplets, Amanda, and Granger, erase it away.

But the world doesn't work that way, does it? There is no light without darkness. No joy without sorrow. No rich when there are no poor. And if we are to have any good in the world it stands to reason that there *will* be evil to counterbalance the Universe.

It's why I became a cop. I make the differences I'm able to make, from sucker-punching a lesser boxer so that he places his ego in check and becomes a better cop (and lives longer) to looking the other way when my brain wants to put together two and two and come up with a 2006 Ford Explorer, found with stolen license plates—one that a witness saw drive away from the murder scene and who described a familiar face to a sketch artist.

There come moments in every life where priorities cry to be shifted, when a man or woman must look into their core and come away with an answer with which they can live. Too often, however, something that can be tolerated in the present festers over the years until it becomes something too cancerous to contain.

Which oath supersedes which? How far do our earthly commitments push us toward decisions that affect things like family and what exactly does justice look like, other than a blind, shape-shifting temptress, at best?

Em, well, she's recovering. Slowly. She still holds on to my badge. Cleaves to it, actually. I ordered another one. Shackleford is much more like himself these days and harassed me ruthlessly, as if I were a rookie who didn't know his ass from his ear.

Em is also remembering more and more about Idaho. She's lost her stomach for wanting to return there, though I've promised her whenever that changes—and I am certain it will—that I will take her there myself and that it will, despite her fears, be a healing experience.

The biggest news is, after getting the okay from Amanda, I asked Em if she would do us the honor of living with us until she gets her GED, picks a college, and allowing us to help her pay for it and get her life started in the direction it should have in the beginning, before the horror, before the unraveling of the plausible.

She said yes, but only if we would adopt her and change her last name to Macaulay. I had planned to broach that subject, too, and was happy that it was what Em wanted. I hadn't been lying to her in the woods when I told her I meant to protect her as my own daughters.

Of course there was a hitch. There's always a hitch when women are involved. They see things clearer than do we cavemen.

"You know she's too attached to you," Amanda reminded me when I told her. "I'm certain I don't need to quote the psychological profiling of a million rescued hostages to you."

I said I didn't care. That Em, like everyone else, would heal, and that as far as I was concerned, she was our daughter now and the rest of it was just shit you deal with when you have children. Amanda agreed, of course. She loves Em, too, and like me is heartbroken that such a wonderful child (and now young woman) should face life alone.

I also shared my plans of retirement with my wife and told her she better start looking for a more challenging job in the Bureau. I'm pretty sure that made the adoption thing go over a little more smoothly, although I don't think Amanda really wants me to retire if that's what it takes to get back to doing what she loves.

In all honesty I'm on the fence. I love being a cop and I don't know what else I could do, even just for fun. I have my twenty years in, so the pension will be there. But as some believe, the minimum is never enough.

J. Lubbock once said:

Rest is not idleness, and to lie sometimes on the grass under trees on a summer's day, listening to the murmur of the water, or watching the clouds float across the sky, is by no means a waste of time.

I don't mind watching a cloud or two, nor listening to the murmur of a stream, but lying down reminds me too much of green pastures.

And then I start thinking about the valley of the shadow of death.

The world needs shepherds.

Afterword

This is my first Afterword, but this is also the first book I've written that ends a trilogy. The reason for this is twofold:

1) I love Detective Bobby Mac, as do many readers. He is a police character and a human being I enjoy writing as he is representative of so many. He is flawed, he is a man's man, he is heroic but also knows what it is to need vengeance. I will likely write more Bobby Mac books one day, perhaps soon. But that brings me to the next reason:

2) I added the paranormal, Good versus Evil, horror-like aspect to this series because I wanted to produce something a little different, but in crossing genres I've had mixed reactions. From more than a few writers I respect, they believe the paranormal aspect, as I refer to it, breaks my "brand" as a Mystery/Detective writer. From readers I respect (and they count most), I have received reviews that imply the series would be better without the "hocus-pocus".

What I meant to add to this series was not traditional, mainstream Paranormal/Horror (e.g. Zombies, Werewolves, Vampires) but rather a very real-world God/Devil, Good/Evil element and to examine the "what if" a police officer found out he was really part of something larger than just him or his own generation but rather a millenniums-long struggle tied to his family name.

On my main webpage, I am going to add a survey link for readers. I'd really like to know what YOU think. I am a bit on the fence. The series does well and is well-reviewed overall, but that doesn't mean it can't be even better. Here is the link, if you are willing to voice your opinion to help me decide which direction (if any) to go:

http://www.surveymonkey.com/s/DLJCW8Q

Acknowledgements

To my proofreader, beta reader, friend, confidant, and most importantly to the book, an honest reader and commenter, Gail Gentry. Like an editor, you always have the perfect suggestions and your proofing is eagle-eyed. Your forthcoming novel will show the world how much talent you've been gifted.

To my wife, Amy, who has read every novel I write more times in full and in part than any other living human being, thank you for believing in me but most for being by my side. The further we get in this journey to that porch swing the more I depend on you and you have supported my dream from the beginning. I love you.

And to the readers. I've said it before but will continue to reaffirm it: you are the lifeblood to the writer. And for me, every letter, each word, all the pages—they are ultimately for you. When you humble authors by reading their work and further by telling others, you literally help the writer survive to write another day. You are so very much appreciated.

About The Author

R.S. Guthrie lives in Colorado with his beautiful wife, three Australian Shepherds, and a Chihuahua who believes she's a forty-pound Aussie. The Guthrie dogs are their children and there is no disputing the fact that the canines rule the household.

Reckoning is the third in the *Detective Bobby Mac Thriller* series, **Black Beast** and **LOST** preceding it. The author's next planned book is the fourth in the *James Pruett Mystery* series, entitled **Aryan Land.** But somewhere in the near future, there is a dog book digging to get out, and it will pay homage to the kindest, most loyal animals on the planet.

Pictured with the author is three year-old Elsa. She is as intelligent and as beautiful as she appears (and knows it all too well).

You can visit him and find out what's next at http://www.rsguthrie.com or read his thoughts on writing (and once in a while other topics) at http://robonwriting.com (also linkable from the main author webpage).